D1565515

DEADLINE

Other books by Cynthia Danielewski:

Still of the Night
Night Fire
Night Moves
Realm of Darkness
Dead of Night
After Dark
Edge of Night

DEADLINE
·
Cynthia Danielewski

Published by Thomas Bouregy & Co., Inc.
160 Madison Avenue, New York, NY 10016

Library of Congress Cataloging-in-Publication Data

Danielewski, Cynthia.
  Deadline / Cynthia Danielewski.
      p. cm.
  ISBN 978-0-8034-9988-1 (hardcover)
  1. Police—New York (State)—Fiction.   2. Reporters and
reporting—Fiction   3. New York (State)—Fiction.   I. Title.
  PS3604.A528D425 2009
  813'.6—dc22

                                        2009025443

PRINTED IN THE UNITED STATES OF AMERICA
ON ACID-FREE PAPER
BY HADDON CRAFTSMEN, BLOOMSBURG, PENNSYLVANIA

Chapter One

Frank Finnegan ran a weary hand through his short brown hair as he stared at the computer screen and finished proofreading the story that he had just written for his job as a reporter with *The Chronicle*. The deadline for the piece was ten o'clock that evening, and a quick glance at his watch assured him that he had completed his assignment with a few minutes to spare. Removing his wire-framed eyeglasses, he pinched the bridge of his nose and pushed his chair back from his desk as he stretched his legs. He was exhausted.

He had been up and about since six o'clock that morning covering an early press conference involving city officials, and he was more than ready to call it a day. Most of his coworkers had already left, and only a few people were in the building. Deciding that he had done enough work for one day, he e-mailed a copy of his story to his editor before he shut down his computer.

Rising from his chair, he removed his tie that he had loosened earlier and placed it on his desk before he began gathering the documents that he would be taking home with him. A reporter's sources were sacred, and he never took any chances when it came to protecting them. He was in the process of closing his briefcase when he heard a thud behind him. He turned swiftly, expecting to see a member of the cleaning crew emptying trash cans, but there was no one there.

"Hello," he called out, waiting for someone to answer. When there was no response, he glanced around the area while listening intently, trying to determine if someone was in the room with him. The height of the gray walls of the cubicles that divided the work spaces of his colleagues prevented him from seeing anybody, but he also couldn't detect any sound except the steady hum of the air conditioner as it fought to control the heat of the hot summer night. With one final glance around, he shrugged off the sound as just the building settling and locked his briefcase before pocketing the key.

He reached for the can of soda that he had started earlier, and finished the remaining liquid in several large gulps. Crushing the can in one hand, he threw it into the trash before slinging his suit jacket over one arm and stuffing his tie into the front pocket of his shirt. With one final look at his desk, he picked up his briefcase and left the room.

He had just pushed the call button on the elevator and was rocking back on his heels waiting for it to arrive when he noticed someone approaching him in his peripheral vision. Before he could turn around to greet the person, a tight cord was wrapped around his throat, cutting off his flow of oxygen.

He dropped his briefcase and suit jacket as panic set in. Reaching up, he struggled with his assailant while he tried to contain the fear that was overtaking him. The relentless force around his throat was making him lightheaded, and he fought valiantly with his assailant as he tried to release the crushing grip. As the noose around his neck continued to tighten, his world faded to black.

Chapter Two

New York police detective Jack Reeves placed his pen on his desk and leaned back in his chair as he read through the report he had just completed. Earlier that evening, he and his police partner, Ryan Parks, had arrested the man responsible for killing a local convenience store clerk, and he was just finishing the final paperwork. He was more than ready to head home to his wife, Ashley, and his son, John. He had spent very little time with either of them this past week as he and Ryan closed in on the man responsible for murdering the clerk, and he was looking forward to spending some serious quality time with his family. Pushing a weary hand through his short black hair that was showing signs of gray, he rose to his feet and was just reaching for his suit jacket when Ryan appeared in the doorway of the detectives' room.

Jack glanced over at him, noticing that Ryan looked as tired as he felt. The deep crow's-feet around his eyes were more pronounced after their long day, and his long gray–streaked brown hair that he wore unconventionally in a ponytail was starting to come loose from the band that secured it. But it was Ryan's demeanor that caught Jack's full attention. Normally a laid-back, easygoing individual, Ryan's body was tense, his facial expression serious as his eyes focused on Jack.

"What's wrong?" Jack asked.

Ryan didn't immediately answer. Instead his eyes went to the suit jacket that Jack was beginning to shrug into. "I hope you don't have any plans to leave yet," Ryan said as he ran a hand across his neck.

Jack's brown eyes narrowed. "Why?"

"We just got a call from *The Chronicle* that one of their reporters was found dead in the building. He was murdered."

Ryan's statement caught Jack's full attention. His wife, Ashley, had been a reporter at *The Chronicle* when they first met, and had maintained the position until the birth of John. "Do we have an identity on the victim?"

"Frank Finnegan."

The name caused Jack to pause. He had met Finnegan on several occasions when he had gone to functions with Ashley, and he had never been overly impressed with the man's arrogant disposition. "I know him. He was a colleague of Ashley's. How was he killed?"

"He was strangled. His body was found by the elevator with a telephone cord wrapped around his neck."

"The guy had a reputation for being cold, ruthless, and calculating when covering his stories," Jack revealed, recalling what his wife Ashley had told him.

"Which means he may have had a lot of enemies."

"According to Ashley, he had a fair share. At least he had when they worked together."

Ryan grunted at the statement. "We need to get over there as soon as possible. Several squad cars are already on their way to secure the premises and the crime scene investigators are being dispatched as we speak."

"What about Ed?" Jack asked, referring to Captain Ed Stall. He knew that Ed had left the precinct about thirty minutes earlier.

"I called him on his cell phone. He'll meet us there."

"Then let's head out," Jack said, picking up his car keys and heading toward the door.

"Is Ashley expecting you home?" Ryan asked as he walked beside Jack.

"She is, but I'll call her from the car and let her know that I won't be there any time soon."

"Do you want me to drive?"

"I will. I'll drive you back later to pick up your car."

Fifteen minutes later, Jack drove into the parking lot of *The Chronicle.* The flashing blue lights of several squad cars illuminated the dark night, and some of the crime scene investigators had already arrived and were beginning to unpack their vans to begin their search.

Jack parked the car and turned off the engine while his eyes took in the organized activity before him. "It looks like the CSI team has enough people to get a thorough search under way."

"Yeah," Ryan agreed as he released his seatbelt buckle. "The rest of the members that were on standby should be arriving shortly."

Jack opened his car door and stepped out. "Let's head in and see what we're dealing with."

Ryan walked beside Jack to the entrance of the building, and after flashing their badges to the uniformed officer guarding the door, they walked inside and noticed that the lobby had several people sitting in the waiting area. All had anxious expressions on their faces.

"Are these the people that were working tonight?" Jack asked one of the officers standing off to the side, while his eyes searched the room.

"Yeah," the officer responded.

Jack grunted. He couldn't help but notice the mannerisms of the people who were being detained for questioning. Most were clearly nervous about the situation they found themselves in, but there was one woman in particular that caught Jack's attention. And that was because she appeared to be totally devastated.

He took a moment to study the woman as she sat on the edge of a chair, her small frame shaking harshly with sobs. His eyes took in her shoulder-length brown hair that hung like a curtain around her face, and her hazel-colored eyes that glistened with uncontrollable tears. He realized that there was something vaguely familiar about her. He knew that he had met her before. Searching his memory, he tried to recall where it was when he suddenly realized that she was an administrative assistant that had worked at the newspaper during the time that Ashley had. Her name was Susan Myers. She had been with the newspaper for well over ten years. And though Jack knew that everybody reacted differently in situations like this, he found her reaction just a bit extreme. He couldn't help but wonder what ties Myers had to Finnegan.

"We're going to begin the interview process shortly," the officer said, bringing Jack's attention back to him. "They're in the process of setting up the conference areas now."

"Where's the victim?" Jack asked.

"Fourth floor."

"That's where his office was located?"

"Yeah."

"Thanks," Jack said, and with one final look at Myers, he and Ryan made their way to the elevator.

"Did you notice how upset the woman in the black suit seemed?" Ryan asked as he walked beside Jack.

"I did."

"I wonder who she is."

"Her name is Susan Myers. When Ashley worked

here, she was an administrative assistant. It'll be interesting to see what information she can lend to this investigation."

"Based on the people being detained, it doesn't look like there were many people in the building tonight. At least workers," Ryan observed.

"There's ten in the lobby. Frank Finnegan makes eleven," Jack said aloud as the elevator arrived on the fourth floor and the doors opened to reveal the first glimpse of the victim.

Jack stepped out of the elevator and immediately reached for a pair of latex gloves from the box that one of the technicians had placed near the body. He pulled them on while he studied the lifeless form before him. His eyes took in the bluish cast to the man's skin, the spiraled phone cord wrapped tightly around his neck, and the way Finnegan lay in a slightly skewed position, not far from the elevator doors. His legs were bent at an awkward angle, and his arms were loosely sprawled by his sides.

Bending down, Jack reached out and touched the cord around Finnegan's neck, noticing that the coated wire had dug into the man's skin, leaving noticeable abrasions. As he stood and continued to look at the man, it wasn't hard to determine that the man had been killed while waiting for the elevator.

Looking down the hallway, Jack noticed the exit sign posted above a stairwell. A quick glance in the opposite direction revealed the same sight. "With the elevator and the two stairwells, there are at least three possible escape routes on this floor for the killer to have utilized," he murmured aloud as Ryan knelt and performed his own examination of the body.

"So the question is, how many entrances are there for someone to gain access to the building from the outside?" Ryan asked.

"Five," a voice answered gruffly, announcing the arrival of Captain Ed Stall.

Jack turned, his eyes locking with Ed's piercing pale-blue eyes that stood out in sharp contrast beneath his thick gray eyebrows and full head of gray hair. "Hey," Jack greeted, "I was wondering when you were going to show."

Ed grunted, and the action made his austere features seem more formidable. Bending down, he pulled on a pair of latex gloves to inspect the victim. "I was in the process of meeting my wife for a late supper when Ryan called. I had to make sure she was okay before I took off." He pulled slightly on the cord wrapped around Finnegan's throat. "Whoever did this used a lot of force."

"I noticed that," Jack said as several crime scene investigators began canvassing the area looking for clues. Moving slightly to allow one of the technicians to pass with a cumbersome tool kit, he asked, "You mentioned there were five entrances. Where are they?"

"All on the first floor. Two of them are loading docks, so there's a possibility that one of those was used as an entrance or exit. I have some people reviewing the security tapes now to see if there's anything that looks suspicious."

"What about the logs from security? We need to make sure that the people in the lobby are the only workers scheduled to be here," Jack said.

"I already put in the request," Ed assured him before asking, "You were scheduled for a day off tomorrow, weren't you?"

"I was," Jack admitted. "But don't worry. Ashley and John will understand that it won't be possible now."

Ed glanced over at Ryan. "And you? Do you have any commitments that you can't get out of?"

Ryan shook his head slightly. "Jane and I were going to go to her parents for dinner, but she'll understand," he responded, making a reference to his girlfriend, Jane Ramsey.

Ed nodded slightly. "I'm glad to hear it. We'll be busy the next few days while we try to get a handle on what happened here tonight. But for now, let's find Finnegan's office and see if there are any clues lying around that will help us make sense of all this."

In the far corner by a large window, Finnegan's desk was being dusted for fingerprints by one of the crime scene technicians. Jack quickly made his way over to the area.

"It looks like he already closed down for the evening," Jack murmured as his eyes took in the dark computer screen, the crushed empty can of soda in the trash basket, and the desk that had literally been cleared of any files or pending work.

"So?" Ryan questioned.

"So, there were no personal belongings by Frank's body. There was no briefcase laying by his side."

"Maybe he didn't have a briefcase with him today," Ryan suggested as he performed his own search of the area.

"Reporters like Frank always carry a briefcase," Jack countered. "He would never have taken any chances with his sources. If he worked anything like Ashley, I guarantee you that he would take home any notes that he considered sacred."

"Maybe he left it in his car."

"Doubtful. He wouldn't have taken any chances with someone gaining access to the information he obtained from his sources."

Ed's brows drew together in a straight line while he contemplated Jack's words. "Meaning you think someone took his briefcase?"

"Unless the person who found him moved it, I would say that's more than a possibility," Jack stated.

"When the call came in, it was called in by the newspaper security director, Brent Jones. The police dispatcher instructed the man to make sure nothing was touched," Ryan said.

"Is he the one who found the body?" Jack asked.

"No. The body was found by the night watchman."

"So we don't know for sure that the area wasn't compromised."

"If the night watchman had any type of experience, he would have known not to touch anything. And the security director assured the police dispatcher that he would make sure that no evidence would be moved."

"Well, hopefully he's a man of his word," Ed said.

Ryan glanced at Ed. "We'll have to take it on faith that he is, until it's proven otherwise."

"I'll have someone search Frank Finnegan's car to see if anything's there," Ed said, reaching for his cell phone to put in the request. After a few moments of conversation, he disconnected the call. "They'll call me the moment they're done. They already identified his car in the lot but it was locked."

"Did they notice any sign of tampering with the car?" Jack asked.

"No. At least nothing obvious. They have a locksmith from the precinct on his way over here now. He should be here shortly."

"The sooner we gain access to the vehicle, the better."

"I think we're all in agreement on that," Ryan said.

Jack glanced briefly at his watch. "When we go downstairs to see how the interviews are progressing, we need to talk to Brent Jones, as well as the guard who found Finnegan," he said, just as one of the crime scene technicians called out that he had found something.

Jack, Ryan, and Ed quickly made there way over to the other side of the room where the shout originated.

"What is it?" Jack asked the moment he was near the technician.

"I think I know where the murder weapon originated from," the technician replied while carefully dusting for fingerprints. "The phone cord is missing from this telephone."

Jack quickly glanced at the desk, noting the vase of fresh flowers that decorated the desktop. But other than that personal touch, the rest of the desk was empty. Taking a few steps back, he glanced at the wall of the cubicle. "The cubicle belongs to Susan Myers."

Ryan's eyes flew to Jack's. "That's the woman that was so upset down in the lobby."

Chapter Three

"Upset?" Ed asked, his full attention immediately caught by Ryan's description of the woman.

"Yeah," Jack responded. "When Ryan and I arrived, she was pretty close to hysterical."

"Did you get a chance to talk to her?"

Jack shook his head and ran a weary hand around the back of his neck. "No. Our first concern was to come up to the fourth floor and see what we were dealing with. And to be honest, I seriously doubt that anybody got any information from Susan Myers yet. The woman seemed barely coherent. The question is, is she upset by Frank Finnegan's murder or by finding herself detained for questioning?"

"You think she could have had something to do with the murder?" Ed asked.

Jack shrugged. "Time will tell. It could just be that she has one of those really emotional personalities. We all know that everybody reacts differently in these types of situations. But the bottom line is that I don't want to leave anything to chance or assumption."

"Then I think talking to her should be one of our first concerns," Ed stated.

"I agree," Ryan said. "But I think it would be a good idea if we hit both Susan Myers and Brent Jones at the same time. It'll give us a chance to cover more ground, as well as eliminate the possibility of them comparing notes."

"What do you have in mind?" Ed asked.

"I'll talk to Brent and Jack can talk to Susan since he's met her before," Ryan suggested.

"She might feel more comfortable talking to someone she knows," Ed acknowledged.

"That's what I thought," Ryan replied. "And to be honest, I'd really like to get Brent Jones's feedback on exactly what transpired here tonight and what the normal operating procedures are for the people that are working late."

Ed nodded. "Sounds like a plan."

"Then let's go downstairs and start talking to everyone," Jack said, turning and leading the way.

When they arrived downstairs, officers were speaking to the individuals that had been detained one on one, leaving enough distance between the people being interviewed to allow for privacy.

"I don't see Susan Myers," Ryan immediately said as he looked around the crowded room.

"Neither do I," Jack replied.

"Where do you think she disappeared to?" Ed asked.

"I'm not sure, but she can't be far. I'm going to go and find her." Jack turned to Ryan. "You'll talk to Brent Jones?"

"I'll do that right now."

"And I'll see if there's anything else that came up with the other people being questioned," Ed said, his gaze encompassing them both. "We'll meet up later and compare notes."

"Sounds good. I'll see you in a while," Jack said as he went in search of Myers.

After talking to the officer assigned to arranging the interviews, Jack located Myers in a conference room behind the security desk. He could hear her harsh sobs as he opened the door, and with a brief nod to the officer who had been assigned to interview her, he let himself into the room and closed the door behind him.

"Susan," Jack greeted.

At the sound of her name, Myers glanced at him with tear-filled eyes. As her body shook on a sob, she asked, "Yes?"

Jack noticed that she had gone through the box of tissues on the table, and he immediately reached for his handkerchief and handed it to her, accepting her mumbled words of thanks. "You probably don't remember me, but we had met on a couple of occasions," he began, when he didn't see any sign that she recognized him. "I'm Jack Reeves, Ashley's husband."

Myers's brow wrinkled slightly before recognition set in. "Of course," she said, her voice breaking on another sob. After several moments, she seemed to get a grip on her emotions. Taking one final shuddering breath, she said, "You'll have to excuse me. Frank's murder is such a shock."

"I know. And if it's okay with you, I'd like to ask you some questions. I know you've been talking to Officer Harris here . . ."

"We haven't actually started the interview process yet," Harris said, his eyes conveying to Jack that Myers had been too upset to talk.

Jack focused back on Myers. "Can we do anything for you? Maybe get you something to drink? Water, tea, coffee?"

"Water," she requested on a shuddering sigh.

Jack nodded. "Would you mind getting it?" he asked Harris.

"Of course not. I'll be right back."

Jack didn't want to wait until the man returned to start the interview. He wanted to get a feel for the woman. An idea of just why she was so upset. "Susan, I know this is extremely unsettling and that you're upset, but we need to determine if you know anything about Frank that would give us a clue as to why he was murdered," he told her gently.

Myers's tears flowed faster at Jack's words, but she was in enough control to shake her head. "No. I mean I know Frank had some personality flaws, but he was basically a good man."

"Personality flaws?"

She hiccupped on a sob. "Frank was a very dedicated reporter. He could be ruthless when covering a story, but that's only because he honestly believed the public had a right to know the truth."

"You liked Frank," Jack said, making note of the way she came to the man's defense. Though she didn't try to hide the fact that people could take exception to the way Finnegan had operated, she also was excusing his actions. Or at least trying to.

"Yes," she practically whispered, reaching up to dry her eyes.

Jack gave her a moment to collect her thoughts. "I know this is hard. We'll take a break any time you need to."

Myers nodded, and after wiping her eyes once more with his handkerchief, she crumpled the square of linen in her hand. "Frank was a good man. A decent man. He didn't deserve this."

Jack refrained from making the comment that nobody deserved this. "I know. And I'm sorry that this happened. But I'm going to need your help to find the person responsible."

Myers nodded again in understanding just as the door

opened and Officer Harris walked in carrying a small bottle of water. He quickly unscrewed the top before handing the bottle to Myers.

Jack waited until she took a few sips. "Susan, can you tell me if Frank did anything different today? Did he mention any problems to you recently regarding a story he was covering? Had anybody threatened him? Did he get any angry phone calls?"

"I don't know," she said softly.

"Think, Susan. This is important. The desks are relatively close together on the fourth floor, and the cubicles don't allow for total privacy. Did you hear Frank arguing with anybody recently?"

"Just Steve."

The casual way she made the simple statement had Jack's full attention. "Steve?" he repeated.

"Steve Akard. He's a reporter."

"What kind of relationship did the man have with Frank?"

Myers took another sip of her water. "They always seemed to be in competition with each other."

"Do you know what they were arguing about?"

"I wasn't really paying attention. They argued on a regular basis."

"Was there any animosity between the two of them?"

Myers shook her head slightly. "I never thought so. They were both just very competitive."

"Competitive? How?"

She was quiet for a moment. "If there was a story that

they both wanted to cover, they didn't always play fair when it came to getting before the editor's desk to get the assignment."

"I don't understand what you mean by that."

Myers nodded slightly and took a deep breath before she began. "There was one instance where Steve was assigned to cover a story that Frank wanted. Frank went out and got certain details on the story from one of his sources and presented them to the editor. The editor reassigned the story to Frank because he thought Frank would do more justice to the piece based on the resources he had in place."

"And Steve didn't take too kindly to that," Jack deduced.

"No. Steve already had the same information as Frank. But because he didn't think Frank would go behind his back like that, he never bothered to keep the editor informed of his progress. He thought he would do that at the editorial meeting the next day."

"And once the story was reassigned, he couldn't get it back?"

"No. The editor, Sam Jenkins, wasn't interested in the games that Steve and Frank played. He said there were enough important stories that needed to be covered to go around, and he didn't want to get involved in any petty squabbles."

"Which didn't help Steve and Frank's relationship," Jack guessed.

"No."

"How long ago did this take place?"

"The first time was several years ago."

"First time? This happened more than once?"

"Yes. But they were both guilty of it." She looked at Jack with misty eyes. "You have to understand that I really think it was more of a game between the two of them. I don't think either of them meant any harm."

"Why do you say that?"

"They have a long history together. They were college roommates."

Jack found that bit of information interesting. "How did they end up working for the same newspaper?"

Myers gave a delicate shrug. "Like I said, they were always in competition. They both applied at the newspaper at the same time. Frank got the original job offer, and when another opening presented itself, Steve jumped at the chance to get in."

Jack considered what she had just revealed, and he knew he had another suspect to add to the list. Because whether or not Myers thought there was any true animosity between the men, Jack suspected there was. But rather than dwell anymore on the working relationship between Akard and Finnegan, he changed the subject to get a better feel for what happened that day.

"What can you tell me about Frank's schedule today?" he asked.

Myers had calmed down considerably while she had been talking, and though she was still obviously upset, she was no longer sobbing. She wiped a few more stray tears. "I know he had an early morning meeting for a press conference for the new city council official, Mike Smith."

"How early?"

Susan's forehead creased in a frown as she tried to recall the time. "Maybe just before six o'clock this morning. I remember because he had called me at home last night to get the address of where the press conference was being held. There was a change of venue, and Frank had been out of the office when we were notified. I had left him a message on his answering machine to call me when he got in."

"Was that unusual for you to do?"

"No. All of the reporters count on me to ensure that they have the correct information. I'm sure I don't have to tell you that one missed press conference can kill a reporter's reputation."

Jack was well aware of that. He had enough experience with Ashley even before they started dating to know that her reputation as a reporter was tied to her ability to break a story before any of the competition did. "I'm sure the newspaper appreciates your dedication."

"I do what I can."

Jack nodded slightly in acknowledgement. "Did you talk to Frank after the press conference?"

"Just briefly. He had promised to buy me lunch in appreciation for the update, but he had the chance to have a one-on-one interview with Mike Smith so he had to take a rain check."

"Did you get a chance to talk to him after that?"

"No."

"You didn't talk at all tonight?" he pressed, finding it hard to believe.

"No. We were going to have a cup of coffee together, but Frank had an unexpected visitor."

"Who?"

"Tom Oden."

The name was familiar to Jack and he searched his memory trying to recall what he could about the man. "He was the city official that had resigned, wasn't he? The one that Mike Smith replaced?"

"Yes."

"Why did he come to see Frank?"

Myers hesitated, her finger absently tracing the rim of the bottle of water, her eyes downcast.

"Susan?" Jack prompted, wondering about her reluctance to speak. "I need all the help you can give me. Any information you reveal will remain confidential," he assured her, in case she had that concern.

"I know."

"Then?"

Myers hesitated only a moment longer. "I'm afraid Frank was partially responsible for Tom Oden having to resign. It was Frank's story that gave life to the scandal that ruined Tom's career and his marriage."

Chapter Four

A short time later, Jack went in search of Ryan and Ed. The two men were standing in the hall talking to a silver-haired man dressed in jeans and a polo shirt. The man's clothes suggested he wasn't working in the building at the time of the murder. He couldn't have been. Jack knew from Ashley's days of working at the paper that they had a dress code, and jeans weren't listed as suitable attire.

"Ryan," Jack called out as he walked over to the small group.

Ryan turned. "Jack, I'm glad you're here. I don't think you've had the chance to meet Brent Jones, the newspaper's security director. Mr. Jones, this is Detective Jack Reeves."

Jack shook the man's hand. "Mr. Jones."

"Detective Reeves," Brent said, returning the greeting.

Jack looked at the man curiously. He looked vaguely familiar, but Jack couldn't place where he had met him. "Have we met before?"

Jones nodded. "We have. Years ago when Ashley worked here."

"You know my wife?"

"I was hired on Ashley's last day here. We met briefly in the hall when you came to help her clean out her desk."

Jack suddenly had a vague recollection of their first meeting. "Of course."

"I'm sorry we're meeting again under these circumstances," Jones said, while running an agitated hand through his hair.

"So am I."

"When I got the call about Frank . . ."

"I imagine it must have been a shock."

"It was. I never thought that when I left here today that something like this would happen."

"What time did you leave?"

"A couple of hours ago."

"You live close by?" Jack asked, inferring from Jones's casual clothes that he had time to go home and change.

"About ten minutes away."

"When was the last time you saw Frank?"

"Around eleven this morning. I had a cup of coffee with him in the break room."

"Did he say anything at that time that suggested he

was having any sort of problems? Did he mention anybody's name?" Jack asked.

"He didn't say a word. As a matter of fact, we were talking about our weekly card game that was coming up."

Jack's eyes narrowed slightly. "You socialized with Frank Finnegan?"

"Yes. Frank and I played cards with a group of people from the newspaper."

"Who else played?"

Jones shrugged. "A few people from pre-press, another reporter, one of my security guards."

Jack considered the information. He couldn't help but wonder if there was any animosity with someone in the card group toward Finnegan. "When was the last time you played?"

"Last Tuesday."

"And everything seemed normal?"

"Yes. We didn't play for high stakes, the games were more of a social nature, but Frank seemed perfectly normal. He didn't mention any problems, or anybody who gave him a hard time."

"Would he have mentioned any problems?" Jack asked, wondering just how close the group actually was.

"A lot of the guys used the game as a sounding board. If they were having problems at home, or with their girlfriend, it was mentioned."

"And as far as you were aware . . ."

"There was nothing. At least not from my personal interaction with the man."

Jack heard the underlying meaning behind the words. "Meaning there's something you're concerned about?"

"Yes."

"What?"

It was Ryan who answered Jack's question. "Mr. Jones reviewed the video surveillance and noticed that a local contractor by the name of Drew Kaye paid Frank a visit today."

"Was he listed on the visitors' log?" Jack asked, knowing that all of Finnegan's visitors would be interviewed.

"He never checked in," Jones answered. "Frank met him in the lobby. The time stamp on the video showed it to be about four-forty-five P.M."

Jack frowned as he addressed Jones. "How were their demeanors?"

"They looked like they were arguing," Jones answered.

"And you're basing that on . . ."

"The angry hand motions of Drew."

Jack studied Jones carefully, trying to determine if he knew more than what he was saying. The no-nonsense expression on the man's haggard-looking features, the silver-gray hair that was sheared close to his head, and the authority in the man's voice were indications that the man took his job seriously. "Do you know if Frank had any problems with Drew Kaye?"

Jones hesitated a moment. "I heard rumors that Drew Kaye held Frank personally responsible for the financial trouble his company is in."

"What do you mean by that?"

Jones expelled a small sigh. "Frank wrote a story about possible corruption when Drew was awarded a bid by local government officials. Because of that piece, Drew lost several contracts."

"Is that statement based on fact?"

"It's based on gossip through the local grapevine. And while I usually don't pay any attention to that type of stuff, I have a feeling that there's some truth to it," Jones replied.

"Was that the same article that accused Tom Oden of corruption?" Jack asked, recalling what he learned from Susan Myers.

"Yes."

"How long was Drew talking to Frank today?"

"Well, that's the problem. We have him on tape until five o'clock, but then we lost track of him," Jones admitted. "We have a lot of employees that leave at exactly five o'clock on the dot. Somewhere in the commotion of the mass exit, Frank and Drew stepped out of the camera's view."

"Meaning that Drew could have made his way into the building through the lobby without checking in at the security desk," Jack stated grimly.

"Yes."

"Did you check with the security guard who was on duty at the time? Did he notice anything?"

Jones grimaced. "Unfortunately, our security guard

posted in the lobby also changes shifts at five o'clock. I already spoke with the guard that had replaced him, but he didn't notice anything."

"What about the one who was working up until five?" Jack asked.

"After speaking to Detective Parks and Captain Stall, I called him at home to see what he had to say."

"And?"

Ryan took it upon himself to answer. "He doesn't have any information that will help with the investigation."

Jack glanced over at Ryan. "You spoke to him?"

"Yeah. He said there were a lot of people around, but he didn't notice or overhear anything that was suspicious."

Jack looked back at Jones, recalling the man's comment that Finnegan and Kaye appeared to be arguing. "How observant is the guard in question?"

"He's usually pretty good, but he's been having some problems at home. It's the only explanation I can think of as to why he didn't notice anything suspicious when the two men met."

Jack was quiet for a moment before asking, "Do you mind if I look at the tape in question?"

"Of course not. Follow me," Jones said, turning and leading the way.

Jack followed Jones into a small surveillance room surrounded by real-time feed monitors, aware that Ryan and Ed were right behind him. He observed the activity in the building on one of the monitors for a moment before his attention was diverted to the small screen off to the right. It was the monitor that was replaying the surveillance tape from the lobby at around 5:00.

"Give me a moment, and I'll get to the time frame that you're interested in," Jones said. Quickly rewinding the tape, he started to play it again for Jack. "You can see Frank Finnegan and Drew Kaye speaking in this frame," he explained, pointing.

Jack studied the video, noticing that Jones was correct in his earlier observation. The two men appeared to be arguing. "You don't have any sound?" he asked.

Jones grimaced. "Unfortunately, no. We never thought it would be necessary."

"Until now," Jack murmured, watching as several people converged into the lobby at once and Finnegan and Kaye disappeared from view.

"Until now," Jones agreed.

"Are there any other tapes that we should look at? Were there any from the fourth floor where the body was found?"

"We don't have cameras up there."

Jack spared him a quick glance. "Why's that?"

"Unfortunately, something like this happening was the last thing we expected. We always counted on our security crew to ensure that nobody got into the elevator that wasn't authorized to be."

"Except that method didn't work today," Jack pointed out, his attention refocused to the tape.

"No, it didn't. And I guarantee you that after what

happened here tonight, our security will be heightened."

"What about the stairwells on the fourth floor? No cameras in those areas either?"

"No. Our cameras are all confined to the first floor. All visitors come through the lobby. We've never had any problems before, and unfortunately, that means that we don't have anything documented that might be of assistance."

Jack cast a quick look at Ed. "What did you find out? Did any of the employees out in the lobby notice anything or anyone?"

"No. Nothing that they paid any attention to anyway."

Jack nodded and took a step back. "It looks like we have our work cut out for us."

"I'll help in any way I can," Jones assured him.

"We appreciate that. We're grateful for your assistance. You've been very helpful."

"Do you have any other questions that I can answer?"

"Not right now."

"Then if there's nothing else at the moment, I have some business to attend to," Jones said.

"Of course."

"If you need me, the guard at the front desk can page me."

"Thanks," Jack said.

"So what did you think?" Ryan asked the moment Jones was out of immediate earshot.

"He seemed genuinely interested in helping," Jack said, his eyes on the surveillance tape.

"I thought so too."

"I don't like the fact that we lost track of Drew Kaye," Ed said.

"Me neither," Jack said. "If the man had an issue with Frank Finnegan, there's always the chance that it was enough of one for him to commit murder. Especially if he blamed Frank for his financial troubles. Money has a way of making people react in extreme ways. But we also have three other people of interest."

"Who?" Ryan asked.

"Tom Oden, Steve Akard, and Susan Myers."

"Akard? Isn't he a reporter?" Ed asked.

"Yes. And a rival of Frank Finnegan's."

"Professional rivalry doesn't necessarily translate to murder," Ed pointed out.

"True. But it's still something we need to look into. We need to determine whether there was any animosity there. Any malice."

"And Oden?" Ryan asked. "Why is he a person of interest?"

"The story Frank Finnegan wrote about corruption between Tom Oden and Drew Kaye caused the breakup of Oden's marriage. The story also ruined his career. I'll fill you in on the details later, but for now, we need to run background checks on all three of the men, as well as Susan Myers. Since it was her phone cord that was used to murder Frank, I want to make sure that she had no hidden agenda against the man."

"We should have the preliminary background reports by tomorrow morning on all of them," Ed assured him. "By the way, we came up empty on the search of Finnegan's car, but I dispatched a search team to his home. Maybe there will be something there that will help us find a motive. If we can pin that down, it'll be easier to narrow down our list of suspects."

Jack nodded. "When I get home, I'll talk to Ashley," he promised. "Maybe she'll be able to shed some light on this from her days of working here."

"It's as good a place as any to start looking for answers," Ed said before looking over at Ryan. "Is there anyone else that you think we should add to the list of immediate suspects?"

"Not right now."

"Good. Then since the coroner already removed the body, let's get everything wrapped up here and call it a night."

Chapter Five

It was almost four in the morning when Jack let himself into the house. Carefully closing the front door so that he wouldn't wake Ashley and John, he locked the deadbolt before making his way into the kitchen that was illuminated by the stove's overhead light. He threw his suit jacket over the back of one of the kitchen chairs and walked over to the refrigerator. He was just reaching for a carton of orange juice when he heard Ashley's voice behind him.

"I was wondering when you were going to get home," she told him softly as she flicked on the kitchen light.

"Hey, babe. I thought you would be sound asleep." Jack poured a glass of orange juice and glanced over at her. He couldn't help but notice that her blond-highlighted hair was slightly tousled, evidence that she had at least made

35

an attempt at getting some sleep. But he could tell by the dark circles under her eyes that the effort had failed.

Ashley raked a hand through her tumbled locks. "You're joking, right? One of my old coworkers is murdered in the building I used to work in, and you expected me to be sleeping soundly?"

Jack grimaced. He should have known better than to make such an assumption. Ashley thrived on news. Her curiosity was one of the traits that made her such a great reporter. Though she had walked away from the position when she had been pregnant with John, he knew that she had never lost her love of news.

Ashley walked over to the small kitchen table and took a seat. Propping her chin up in her hand, she asked, "So what do you know so far?"

Jack inwardly sighed. He should have known that Ashley would cut right to the chase. Though he honestly wanted to talk to her about the case, Frank Finnegan in particular, he was also exhausted and would seriously have no problem falling asleep. But he could tell by his wife's demeanor that the option wasn't going to be available to him. At least not yet. He lifted the carton of orange juice for her inspection. "Want a glass?"

"No, thanks."

Jack nodded and put the carton back into the refrigerator before walking over to the table. Placing his glass on the table, he loosened the knot of his tie while he hooked a foot around the leg of the chair directly opposite her, and pulled it out. "I don't have much to tell you," he warned.

"I might be able to help."

"I know. And I did want to talk to you about that."

"Then . . ."

Jack studied her silently before asking, "Aren't you tired?"

"Exhausted. But I'm not going to be able to sleep until we talk."

Jack would have laughed, but what happened was no laughing matter. And he knew Ashley was totally serious. Deciding that now was as good a time as any for them to talk, he took a sip of his juice before asking, "What can you tell me about Frank Finnegan?"

Ashley didn't hesitate. "He's a good reporter."

"I know. But if I remember correctly, he was also a difficult person to get along with. At least that's what you had told me at one time."

Ashley nodded. "That's true. And that hasn't changed since I left my post."

"What makes you say that?"

"You know I still keep in touch with my old coworkers. I hear things."

Jack's eyes narrowed slightly at the vague answer. "Like what?"

"Like how Frank and another reporter by the name of Steve Akard were up to their old tricks."

Ashley's mention of Akard had Jack looking at her

curiously. Susan Myers had mentioned the man's name to him, and he couldn't help but wonder what the man's true relationship with Finnegan was. "What do you mean that they were up to their old tricks?"

"Just that they were always in competition with one another. From what I heard, Frank was working on a story about corruption with a local government official, and Steve took exception to him getting the byline."

"Why?"

"Because Steve broke the story first. He had called and left a message for the editor that he was coming in to speak to him about it, but somehow Frank got to the editor first and convinced him that the story was his idea. The incident was just another brick in the wall between the two men."

"You wouldn't by any chance know how Frank managed to pull that off, would you?"

Ashley hesitated. "I heard through the grapevine that Susan Myers may have played a role in it."

Jack was curious about Ashley's choice of words. "Played a role? Why would she do that?"

Ashley gave a delicate shrug. "Because it was rumored that she was romantically involved with Frank."

Jack sat back in his chair. "Susan Myers was romantically involved with Frank Finnegan?" The news hadn't previously been brought up by anyone that evening. And that bothered Jack. He now had a good understanding of why Myers had been so upset when he and Ryan had arrived at the newspaper. But he didn't understand why she didn't admit to the relationship when he had spoken to her. That bothered him. His experience told him that the only time people withheld information was if they were trying to avoid any connection to the crime. If what Ashley said was true, there was now a lot of suspicion that could be focused on Myers. "Are you sure that she was involved with Frank?"

"That's what the rumor mill was saying. And I have to say, I wasn't that surprised when I heard about it."

"Why's that?"

"There was always some tension between the two of them when I worked there."

"What kind of tension?"

"A certain flirtatiousness. A lot of people just assumed that there was something going on between the two of them."

"Including you?"

"Yes."

Jack contemplated her words. "Was it just speculation?"

Ashley paused. "If you're asking me if they ever went public with their relationship, I would have to say no. But everybody knew that something was going on. And from what I was told last week when I was speaking to my friend Karen down at the paper, things were a little rough between the two of them."

"Rough?"

"Tense."

"Any idea on the reason why?"

Ashley shrugged. "From what I heard, Frank showed up at the office one day with a beautiful woman on his arm, and couldn't resist flaunting her in front of Susan. Someone later saw Susan crying in the ladies room. And since it was right after Frank left . . ."

"They just assumed it had to do with his companion that day," Jack concluded grimly.

"Yes."

"I spoke with Susan Myers when I went to the news-paper."

"She was there?"

"Yes. She was very upset."

"That doesn't surprise me, but her being there does."

"Why?"

"Because when I worked at the newspaper, Susan left work at five o'clock every night."

"Maybe she had to work late last night."

"Maybe, but it's doubtful."

"Why do you say that?"

"Because Susan has a part-time job. She works Monday through Friday night at the community college."

"Maybe she quit her part-time job."

Ashley shook her head. "She wouldn't do that. She needed the money. She helps her parents out financially. They have a lot of medical bills, and they depend on whatever money Susan sends them."

"How do you know that?"

"Susan mentioned it years ago. And since I know that

her parents are still alive, it makes sense that she would continue to contribute financially to them."

"I guess I'll be paying another visit to Susan to find out just why she didn't mention any of this."

"Can I ask how Frank was murdered?"

Jack debated on whether or not to reveal the information, but he knew it would be all over the news tomorrow. "He was strangled outside his office."

"With what?"

"Susan Myers's telephone cord."

Ashley's eyes widened. "I can't imagine that Susan had anything to do with Frank's murder."

"Why? Because she had feelings for the man? You've covered enough homicide stories to know that the relationship itself dictates that she's a person of interest in the investigation. Especially if there were problems."

Ashley couldn't deny Jack's words. "I would guess that a lot of people had problems with Frank."

"I agree with you. And we have several other people of interest that we'll be investigating."

Ashley was quiet for a moment before saying, "If you want my help with anything, all you have to do is ask."

"I know. And I appreciate that."

"I mean it, Jack. I can help. I have enough contacts down at the newspaper to get you answers."

"I know you do. And to be honest, I'll probably be taking you up on that offer."

"Good."

"It looks like I'll be working long hours until we have some answers in this case."

Ashley nodded. "I realize that."

"Are you okay with that?" he felt compelled to ask, knowing that he had been putting a lot of hours in on his job lately.

Ashley smiled slightly in understanding. "As much as I miss you, I know you're only doing your job."

Jack reached for her hand and gently kissed the back of it. "I hate being away from you and John."

"And we hate you being away," she assured him softly. "But I understand. And like I said, if you need me to do anything . . ."

Jack smiled slightly. "I'll let you know." He knew that Ashley would be discreet in obtaining any information.

Ashley returned his smile while her eyes caressed his features, noticing the lines of strain around his eyes. "You look tired."

"I am."

"We should head up to bed."

Jack nodded and drained his glass in one swallow. "Let me just rinse out my glass."

Ashley waited until Jack completed the task before she rose. "What time do you have to be at the station tomorrow?"

"I'd like to be there by noon."

She cast a quick glance at the kitchen wall clock. "At least you'll be able to get some rest."

"Until John gets up," Jack replied with a smile.

Ashley shared Jack's smile at the thought of their son. John was a precocious three year old with boundless energy. "He'll understand that you're tired and need some sleep."

Jack shot her a look. "Are you sure about that?"

Ashley gave a slight laugh. "Not really. But it sounded good."

"If not totally unrealistic."

"John will probably be in our bedroom bright and early wanting to spend some time with you."

"I know."

"I'll try and think of ways to keep him occupied."

"As long as I get five hours of sleep, I should be good. I'd like to spend some time with him before I go in tomorrow. He's growing so quickly, I hate missing out on everything."

"I think we can manage the five hours," she said as she walked beside him to the staircase.

"How was he tonight?" Jack asked as he placed his hand on the small of her back as they walked upstairs.

"He was missing you. He didn't understand why he didn't see you all day."

Jack felt a pang of guilt. He had left the house that morning before John was awake. "I'll have to see if I can make that up to him."

"I'm sure you can."

"And what about you?"

Ashley looked up at him. "What about me?"

"How do I make this up to you?"

"I'll think of something," she teased.

Jack laughed. "I'm sure you will," he said, pausing outside his son's bedroom and peering in. "Sound asleep."

"Just like you should be."

Jack grunted. "Come on. Let's get to bed."

Chapter Six

It was close to noon when Jack made his way into the precinct. Stopping in the break room, he poured himself a cup of coffee before heading to the detectives' room and Ed's office.

Ed was by Ryan's desk when Jack walked in. The two men paused their conversation at his entrance.

"Hey," Jack greeted, looking at the two of them curiously. "Did I miss something?"

"Jack, I'm glad you're here," Ed said.

"What's up?" Jack asked, taking a sip of his coffee.

"Let's go into my office where we'll have a little privacy," Ed directed, turning and leading the way.

Jack followed Ryan into the small office, pausing only long enough to close the door. "So tell me what I

45

missed," he said as he walked over to take a seat in front of Ed's desk.

Ed's chair creaked as he leaned his weight into it. "I got an anonymous tip this morning regarding Frank Finnegan's murder."

"And?" Jack prompted as he leaned forward so he could place his cup on the edge of the desk.

"And apparently Susan Myers was romantically involved with Frank Finnegan."

"I know."

Ed's eyes narrowed. "You know?"

"Ashley mentioned it this morning when I got home. Apparently the two of them had a sort of relationship for quite some time."

Ryan looked at Jack. "Did Susan mention anything about it to you last night when you spoke to her?"

"No. She didn't even hint at it. She gave me the impression that they were friends, but that was all."

Ed picked up a pen and began tapping it on his desk. "So the question is, what is she trying to hide?"

Jack reached for his cup and took another sip of his coffee. "I thought I would track her down today and have another talk with her. I have to admit that it bothered me when I found out that there was more to her relationship with Finnegan than she let on. It bothered me even more to learn that according to one of Ashley's friends down at the newspaper, Finnegan came in last week with an attractive woman on his arm. If he and Susan were seriously involved, and he was flaunting someone else in front of her . . ."

"She may have had a motive to kill him," Ed concluded.

"Revenge?" Ryan asked.

"People do strange things when emotions are involved. The man was strangled. Either a man or a woman would have been able to commit the act. The marks on his neck suggest a lot of force was used, but the telephone cord was thick enough that it would have cut into the skin if enough pressure was exerted. Pressure doesn't necessarily equate with strength."

"I agree with Ed. I think we'd better find out just how close the two of them were. We can head over to her house just as soon as we're through here." Jack looked at Ed. "Can you get us a warrant? If they were involved, it would make sense that there would be things in her home from their relationship. Something might be there that would help us with the case."

Ed nodded. "Consider it done."

"Thanks," Jack said before adding, "Did the crew you sent to Frank Finnegan's house uncover anything?"

Ed sighed. "Not much. They took his files into evidence but it'll take some time to go through them."

"What about the background reports on our other suspects? Did anything show?" Ryan asked.

"Again, not much. At least not much more than we learned last night. The only thing that stood out was that

Susan Myers has a part-time job at a local college. She usually works evenings there, so I was a little curious about why she was working late at *The Chronicle*. But a couple of phone calls answered the questions."

"What did you find out?" Jack asked, recalling Ashley's comments about Susan working evenings at the community college.

Ed shrugged. "It's summer. The hours have been cut back a little. Even though Susan normally works five nights a week there, she was only scheduled to work three nights this week. And according to her supervisor at *The Chronicle,* Susan took some personal time this week. She stayed late yesterday to make up the hours. Copies of the background reports are on your desk. There's also a copy of the article Frank Finnegan wrote on corruption with the city officials. The guy really did a job on Tom Oden and Drew Kaye. He pretty much accused Oden of ignoring the other bids, and accepting Drew Kaye's in exchange for a personal favor that would be financially beneficial."

Jack took note of Ed's comment. "What did we come up with regarding the whereabouts of Steve Akard, Drew Kaye, and Tom Oden?"

"Steve Akard was out of town on assignment late yesterday afternoon," Ed answered.

"Susan Myers claimed to overhear the man arguing with Frank Finnegan earlier that day," Jack said, recalling her statement from the previous night. "Can his whereabouts be confirmed?"

"He checked in at the paper early afternoon, but he left at three o'clock. The security logs support his claim. From all indications, he was supposed to be in the Hamptons covering a political fund-raiser."

"What do you mean he was supposed to be?"

"It means that we have witnesses that saw him there, but not until after ten o'clock in the evening."

"Meaning he could have been in town long enough to murder Finnegan," Jack concluded.

Ed shrugged. "It's possible."

"And being a reporter at *The Chronicle,* he would have known all the entrances and exits of the building," Ryan said.

"As well as where the cameras were located," Jack said, referring to the surveillance cameras set up in the lobby.

"Yes to both comments," Ed said.

"So the man needs to offer us the names of people who could verify what time he arrived at the fund-raiser."

"If he wants to be cleared as a suspect," Ed replied.

Ryan looked at Ed. "And Drew Kaye? Did he give a statement of his whereabouts last night?"

"The officer I sent to speak with him found him at home, sound asleep. The man appeared shocked when he heard of Finnegan's murder."

"Any chance it was an act?"

"I don't know. Anything's possible. He didn't deny seeing Frank in the lobby yesterday. As a matter of fact, he made a point of mentioning it to the officer," Ed told them, reaching for the report he had from the officer who interviewed the man. He glanced through it briefly. "According to the report, he actually mentioned the argument several times."

"In what context?" Jack asked, reaching out to take the report from Ed.

"From my understanding, the statements were just made and randomly dropped throughout the conversation."

Jack finished reading the report, and when he was through, he handed it to Ryan so that he could look at it. "He might have made the statements as a way of drawing attention away from himself," Jack suggested.

"Maybe. Time will tell."

Ryan glanced through the report before placing it back on Ed's desk. "What about Tom Oden? What do we know about him?"

Ed shrugged. "The man has an alibi. He was with family members until eleven last night. I had some officers check with the family this morning, and they all seem to be vouching for his whereabouts."

"Any chance they're covering for him?" Ryan asked.

"There's always that chance. It'll be up to you and Jack to determine if there was any opportunity for him to go to the paper, kill Finnegan, and get back to the family gathering before anyone noticed."

"What kind of gathering was it?" Jack asked.

"It was a family barbecue. And from what I understand, there were over forty people there. Unless the man stayed with one person the whole time, he probably had an opportunity to get away for a while."

"Ryan and I will check it out."

"I'm counting on it. You two do whatever you need to get some answers today. If we're lucky, whoever murdered Finnegan is still unsettled by the act. Maybe the demeanors of our suspects today will help us pinpoint our murderer. Unless the person is totally cold-blooded, he or she has to be feeling some sort of remorse, some unsettlement over committing the act of murder."

"We'll do our best to come up with answers," Jack assured him.

"I know you will. I took the liberty of calling the newspaper before you two arrived. Susan's taking the day off today, so hopefully she'll be at home."

"How long before you'll have the warrant?" Jack asked.

"Give me an hour."

Jack looked at Ryan. "That'll give us enough time to review the information that we have so far. Maybe there's something in the background reports that'll give us some clues."

"Sound good to me," Ryan replied.

"Then you two start sorting through everything and let me get started on getting the warrant. I know a judge that owes me a favor. I'll see if he'll put a rush on it," Ed promised.

Jack nodded and stood before reaching for his coffee cup. "Call us and let us know when it will be ready."

"Count on it," Ed said, watching as the two of them left his office.

"So what do you think?" Ryan asked the moment they were back at their own desks.

Jack finished the remaining coffee in his cup. "I think we have a lot of ground to cover today, and I don't think it's going to be easy to get Susan Myers to talk about her relationship with Frank Finnegan."

"I'm going to agree with you on that one."

"The fact that she didn't mention it at all yesterday leads me to believe that there's something she's covering up. There's something that she doesn't want known. People that go to lengths to keep relationships secret are usually trying to hide something. With any luck, we'll be able to at least determine what that is today."

"She was extremely upset yesterday," Ryan reminded him as he reached for a bottle of water on his desk and took a deep drink.

"Yes, and at the time, we both found that a little strange."

"But now we have an idea of why."

"True."

Ryan placed his bottle on his desk then reached for the folder they had on Myers. "It says here that she worked at the newspaper for ten years."

"Finnegan was at the newspaper for that length of time too."

Ryan looked over at him. "Did Ashley mention how long their relationship was going on for?"

"You mean their alleged relationship?"

"Do you doubt that it existed?"

"No, but so far it's all speculation based on rumor. It's anybody's guess about just how involved they were. But regardless, getting answers isn't going to be an easy task."

Ryan nodded and kicked his legs out in front of him while he finished reading the file. "So what's the game plan for today? Do you think we'll get to everyone?"

"I think we will," Jack said, motioning to the file that Ryan was still reviewing. "Susan Myers's apartment will be our first stop. If we arrange for a search team to come with us, you can direct them and help take the place apart while I question her. Depending on what does or doesn't come out of that interview, we can try and track down Steve Akard and then head over to Tom Oden's. If we have time, we'll stop in at Drew Kaye's office."

"Do you think Akard, Oden, and Kaye will talk?"

"I'm not sure. I guess it's going to depend on how much pressure we put on them," Jack said, reaching for the folder containing the article Finnegan had written. "Ed was right. Finnegan really crucified Oden and Kaye."

Ryan reached for the folder as soon as Jack was through and began reading. "I think Oden and Kaye will talk only if they have nothing to hide. But at least if we get everything done that we need to, we'll have an idea of which direction we'll need to go to get this case solved."

"That's what I'm hoping for."

"It'll be an interesting day at the very least."

"Yeah, it will," Jack agreed.

"I guess it'll be a late night," Ryan said, laying down the folder and leaning back in his chair.

"Ashley's not expecting me home any time soon. What about you? Do you have any plans you can't cancel tonight?"

"No. Jane's having dinner with her parents. She already knows that I'll be working late hours on this case."

"You two have been seeing each other a while now, haven't you?"

"Several years. Why?"

Jack shrugged. "Just wondering if you two had any plans of cementing your relationship."

"We've been talking about it. But we've both been down the marriage road before."

"What does that mean?"

"Just that we want to make sure the next time either of us walks down the aisle that it'll last."

Jack smiled and was about to comment when his phone rang. "Reeves."

After several moments of conversation, he disconnected the call. "The warrant will be ready in thirty minutes. Let's finish reading these reports, and then head over to the courthouse to pick it up."

Chapter Seven

It was almost 2:00 in the afternoon when Jack and Ryan drove into the apartment complex where Susan Myers lived. A few cars were parked in the lot, but the majority of the residents didn't appear to be home.

Jack glanced at Ryan. "What apartment does she live in?" he asked, as his eyes took in the surroundings. Though the buildings were old, they were obviously well maintained. The shrubbery that edged the sides of the buildings was green, lush, and trimmed, and the blacktop of the parking lot had recently been repaved, the potholes from the previous winter filled.

Ryan looked down at the file he held and opened the cover. "Nine A," he said before peering through the windshield. "It should be at the end of this first building."

Jack grunted and drove into an empty parking spot nearest to her door. Several buildings comprised the apartment community, but the parking lot in front of the building that held her unit was all but empty. "I hope she's home," Jack said, looking at the few cars.

"You and me both."

"Let's go."

"Her windows are open," Ryan observed as he and Jack made their way to the front door.

Jack looked at the bay window. "It sounds like she has company," he said as they got closer to her apartment and he heard voices drifting out.

"Maybe she's watching television."

"Maybe." But Jack doubted it. He could have sworn that he heard her voice, and she didn't strike him as the type to talk to herself. Curious about who could be with her, he pressed the lit buzzer on the doorbell.

The voices stopped and it was a few seconds before the distinct sound of footsteps could be heard approaching the door, one set heavy and the other light.

Jack cast a quick look at Ryan. "She's not alone."

"No."

"Who is it?" Myers called out without opening the door.

"Detective Jack Reeves and Detective Parks," Jack replied.

There was a long pause before the door opened to reveal Myers. "Detectives," she said, surprise clearly evident in her voice.

"Susan," Jack greeted, noting that her eyes were still red and puffy from crying. He fought back a wave of sympathy as he turned to introduce Ryan. "You remember Detective Parks from last night."

Myers looked at Ryan and nodded in greeting before she turned back to Jack. "I don't understand why you're here . . ."

"We'd like to talk to you again. Some things were brought to our attention that we need clarification on," Jack said.

Myers shook her head slightly in confusion. "But why didn't you just call? I gave you my phone number last night. I would have been more than willing to talk to you on the phone."

"What we need to talk to you about really can't be discussed on the phone." Jack didn't want to tell her that he wanted the chance to observe her body language when he questioned her on her relationship with Frank Finnegan. "And there's also another reason why we stopped by unannounced."

"What?"

Jack didn't want to beat around the bush. He knew the best way to catch someone off guard was to be forthright and direct. "We have a warrant to search your home." He noticed the way her slight frame tensed, the

way her hazel eyes widened. He knew that his statement had blindsided her.

Myers pushed a trembling hand through her long
brown hair that hung straight by her face. "A warrant?"
she repeated.

"Who is it, Susan?" a male voice rasped loudly as a
tall, burly man with dark-blond hair cropped close to his
head appeared by her side.

Jack sensed that the man had been hovering off to her
side, trying to be unobtrusive. But at his words, Jack took
a moment to look at him. Though his looks were only
vaguely familiar, his distinct voice triggered something
in Jack's memory. He recognized him from a party he at-
tended with Ashley when she had worked for the newspaper. "Are you Steve Akard?"

The man's eyes narrowed. "Have we met?"

"Once," Jack admitted. "I'm Jack Reeves. Ashley's
husband. She was a reporter at the newspaper."

There was a long pause of silence before Akard answered. "Of course," he said, his eyebrows rising slightly
as he placed Jack in his mind. But his slight distraction lasted only a moment. He immediately honed in on
Jack's statement regarding the warrant. "I believe I heard
you say that you had a warrant to search Susan's apartment?"

"That's right," Jack said, feeling Myers's eyes on him,
and sensing her fear. He looked back at her and, reaching into his suit jacket, he pulled out the document.

Myers reached for the warrant with a shaking hand

and read the document before looking up at Jack with wide eyes. "But I don't understand . . ."

Jack knew she was upset by the turn of events, and he sensed that her distress was genuine. He heard the nervous tremor in her voice and noticed her shaking limbs.

Jack glanced at Akard before turning back to Myers. "Perhaps you'd like to talk alone?" he asked.

"No," she said, her hand reaching for Steve's as if seeking moral support.

"If you're sure . . ." Jack gave her the chance to change her mind. He didn't want anybody else around that could influence her answers. But he knew that unless he actually arrested her, he couldn't prevent Akard from sitting in on their meeting. And right now, he wasn't in a position to bring her down to the station.

"I am. Whatever you have to say can be said in front of Steve," she replied, looking at Akard briefly.

Jack sensed that there was some type of communication going on between the two, though no words were spoken. Knowing that there was little he could say at this point that would change her mind, he nodded. "If that's what you want."

"It is," she assured him, relieved that he wasn't pushing the issue. She took a few moments to collect herself before she admitted, "I still don't know why you need to search my apartment."

Jack sensed that it wasn't their visit that was disconcerting her, it was the search warrant. He glanced once more at Akard before turning his attention back to her and saying, "We understand you had a relationship with Frank Finnegan."

"We were friends," Myers acknowledged, looking at Jack with confusion. "I thought I made that clear last night when we spoke."

Jack didn't comment on her last statement, he saw no reason to. Instead he went to the true reason behind his and Ryan's visit. The reason the search warrant was issued. "We understand you were more than friends," he said, while giving the nod to Ryan to start the search.

Myers watched Ryan warily for several moments before her attention refocused on Jack. "What are you looking for? Surely you don't think that I had anything to do with Frank's murder?" she asked, her voice rising.

"Right now we just have a lot of questions that we need answers to," Jack said, not wanting to alarm her.

"But it's not necessary to search my home. I'm willing to cooperate with you. I'll answer any questions you have."

"I appreciate that. But that still doesn't prevent the necessity for us to search your home," he replied, just as he heard the sound of the CSI van as it pulled into the space by his car.

Myers's attention was focused on the crew that was exiting the van before her eyes flew to Jack's. "There's going to be other people searching my home?"

"Yes. And you'll need to give them room to do their job. Is there somewhere we can go to talk?"

Myers closed her eyes briefly. "The kitchen," she said, her hand gripping Akard's hard as she led the way, her knuckles turning white from the pressure she was exerting.

Jack followed, watching the interaction between Myers and Akard. They seemed close. Too close. He couldn't help but think that there was more to their relationship than that of coworkers.

Myers led the way into the kitchen that was separated from the living room by a swinging door. Pushing the doorstop down with the toe of her foot so that she could keep an eye on the proceedings from the search, she walked over to a round oak table. She didn't take a seat, instead she gripped the back of a chair and turned to Jack. "Would you like a cup of coffee?"

"Coffee would be great," Jack responded, knowing that he had to find some way to put her at ease. She was tense, too aware of what was happening in the other room to answer his questions without being on guard.

Myers nodded. "I just brewed a fresh pot. Have a seat and I'll get it," she said, relieved to have something to do.

"Thanks."

"It's no problem," she assured him, though her voice was still a little shaky. She turned to Akard. "Would you mind getting the cups down from the cupboard?"

"No problem," he replied through gritted teeth. When he had retrieved the cups, he came back to the table and looked Jack squarely in the eye. "Should Susan call her attorney?" he asked without preamble, the tone of his voice slightly defensive, his body tensed.

"That's entirely up to Susan," Jack answered, curious about the man's presence. About why he was so defensive.

"Is she under suspicion for Frank's murder?" he asked bluntly.

Myers came back to the table with the coffee. "Am I?"

"Right now, we just need answers," Jack told her truthfully. There was no reason to say that she was a person of interest. He figured she already determined that. His main objective was to get her to relax enough to talk. To answer the questions her relationship with Finnegan posed.

"So you're searching her home?" Akard asked incredulously, not buying Jack's explanation.

Jack knew that he had to get Akard to back down if he wanted Myers to cooperate. The only way he knew how to do that was to make a direct attack. "From our understanding, Susan had a personal relationship with Frank Finnegan," Jack said, repeating his earlier comment since she hadn't acknowledged it. He watched her closely. He didn't miss the flush that came over her face.

"Frank and I were friends. Good friends," she admitted while pouring the coffee.

"Your relationship went beyond that of casual friends."

She hesitated briefly. "Yes, it did."

Jack was glad that she didn't try and deny it. It would have made his job that much harder. "Why didn't you mention the nature of your relationship last night?" he asked after taking a sip of the hot coffee.

There was a long pause. "I didn't think it was important."

"It is. We're investigating the man's murder. Any information may prove pertinent to the investigation."

"I'm sorry. I honestly wasn't trying to withhold information."

Jack didn't respond, he saw no reason to. She would have to explain. She was the only person who could.

Myers's eyes fell away from his stare, and her gaze went to the commotion in the other room. "I still don't understand . . ."

"Why we're searching your home?"

"Yes."

"We might be able to find something that will help us find Frank's murderer. Things that don't necessarily mean anything to you, might prove valuable in solving this case."

Akard frowned at Jack's explanation and looked at Myers. "I think you should call your lawyer."

She shook her head slightly. "No, I have nothing to hide."

"But Sue . . ."

"It's okay, Steve," she said, her voice soft, but firm. "I have nothing to hide from Detective Reeves. If I have any information that would prove helpful, I want to share it."

Akard didn't look happy with her response, but he

didn't argue. After a long pause of silence, he sighed. "It's your choice."

She reached out and covered his hand, her thumb absently stroking his skin. "Thank you."

Jack watched the interaction between the two of them, noticing again how they seemed to be more than just friends. The way she leaned on him for moral support, the protective way he hovered over her, and the simple caress that Myers had bestowed on Akard when she had touched his hand all suggested that there was something else going on between them.

Myers looked back at Jack and she caught the perplexed expression on his face. "You're curious about the relationship between Steve and myself, aren't you?"

"A little."

She looked at Akard once more before turning back to Jack. "I guess there's something you should know."

"What's that?" Jack asked, keeping his expression neutral.

"Steve and I are very close."

"I can see that."

She smiled slightly. "There's a reason for it. You see, Steve and I were engaged when we were just out of high school."

Chapter Eight

"You were engaged," Jack repeated, wrapping his mind around her words and realizing that she had inadvertently revealed a motive for Steve Akard to have killed Frank Finnegan. One that went beyond professional rivalry. If Akard still had feelings for his ex, and Finnegan and Myers were involved, jealousy may have played a part in how Finnegan ended up dead.

"Yes," she responded. "Steve and I were high school sweethearts."

Jack glanced at Akard, noticing that the man was clenching his jaw. The muscle was turning white under the pressure. He sensed that the man was less than thrilled that their secret was out, and he couldn't help but wonder why. He turned his attention back to Myers. "How long were you engaged?"

"Just a year. We realized early on that we had made a huge mistake. But we've remained very close."

"Does anybody down at the newspaper know about your relationship?" Jack asked as he reached for his cup of coffee and took a sip of the hot liquid.

"No. We thought it best to keep it to ourselves. It was nobody's business."

"It still isn't," Akard interjected.

"Unless your relationship is somehow involved with Frank Finnegan's murder investigation, there's no reason for anybody to know. The information will only be revealed if it becomes pertinent," Jack said, making eye contact with both of them.

Myers glanced at Akard and her hand covered his before her attention focused on Jack. "We would appreciate your discretion."

"You have it."

"Thank you."

Jack took another sip from his coffee before directing his next question to Akard. "Do you mind if I ask what your feelings were for Frank Finnegan?"

Akard gave a slight shrug. "Feelings? He was a co-worker. Nothing more. Nothing less."

"Yet from all accounts so far, you shared a professional rivalry," Jack said, not mentioning that Myers was the one who clued him in on that.

"So? Last time I checked, that wasn't a crime."

"True. But did the rivalry extend beyond the newspaper?"

Akard frowned. "What exactly are you asking?"

Jack studied the man quietly for a moment, trying to determine just how much to push. He needed to see if there was any animosity there due to the fact that Finnegan had a relationship with Myers, but he couldn't afford to alienate the guy. He needed his cooperation. "I mean no disrespect by asking this, but did it bother you that Susan and Frank had dated?"

"Why would it?"

Jack looked pointedly at their clasped hands on the table. "You obviously still have feelings for one another."

There was a long pause of silence before Myers took it upon herself to answer on Akard's behalf. "Steve and I are close, but we're not romantically involved. That part of our relationship ended years ago."

Jack looked at Akard. "So Susan having a relationship with Frank Finnegan wouldn't have bothered you?"

"It bothered me, but not the way you mean."

"Could you expand on that?"

Akard's eyes narrowed. "What do you want me to say? That Frank was a lowdown snake who would sell his own soul for a story?"

"Is that what you think?"

"It's the truth."

"And how did you feel about Susan dating him?" Jack pressed.

He hesitated. "I didn't like seeing Susan getting mixed up with a guy like that. But I also knew that it was her life, and I had no right to interfere. All I could do is be there and pick up the pieces," he replied, some of his hostility toward Finnegan seeping into his words.

"Did you pick up the pieces last week?" Jack asked. Myers paled at the question, and Akard's eyes narrowed to mere slits as his jaw clenched.

"What's that supposed to mean?" he asked.

"I understand that Frank Finnegan came into *The Chronicle* last week with a woman on his arm," Jack said, focusing his attention on Myers. He looked for a reaction of some sort, something that would give him a clue as to just how deeply affected she was by Finnegan's lack of tact.

Myers cast her eyes toward the table briefly before meeting Jack's gaze. "Yes, he did."

"Did you know her?"

"Not personally, but I knew of her."

When she didn't offer anything further, Jack asked, "Did you know her name?"

There was a pause. "I did. Her name was Lisa Reyes. She works for a magazine in the city."

"What magazine?" Jack asked, making a mental note of the woman's name.

"The *Bridal Boutique*."

Jack wasn't familiar with the magazine, but he knew it wouldn't be difficult to get an address and phone number. "Was that the first time Frank had brought her to the newspaper?"

"Yes, but it wasn't the first time he had seen her."

"How do you know that?"

"Because I had a huge argument with him on the night that he brought her to the newspaper. And in the heat of the moment, he admitted it."

The way she made the statement told Jack more than words that there was a lot more to their relationship than she had just admitted. "Can I ask what you argued about?"

"Just things."

"Whatever you say will remain confidential."

"It was just stupid things. Nothing important."

Jack doubted that but he didn't press her. He could tell by the offhand way she made the comment that she wouldn't be offering a further explanation. He couldn't help but wonder if her reluctance to speak was stemming from Akard's presence. Deciding to change the subject, he asked, "Just how close were you to Frank, Susan?"

Myers hesitated again. "We saw each other on and off for a few years."

"So the relationship was serious?"

"At one time I thought so. But I realized that Frank was only playing with my emotions."

"What do you mean?" Jack was grateful she was opening up, even if she was being cautious.

She gave a delicate shrug. "Just that I think he saw me as a convenience more than anything else. If he was at loose ends, he would call me. If he was busy, he wouldn't. It's as simple as that."

"That must have hurt," Jack sympathized, wondering

how any woman could put up with being treated that callously.

"It only hurts if you care."

"Are you saying that you didn't?"

Myers shook her head. "No. I can't say that."

"So exactly what are you saying?"

"I'm saying that when I finally understood what Frank was about, it stopped hurting so much. Frank was a selfish individual. Just the fact that he brought a woman into *The Chronicle* and flaunted her in front of me told me everything I needed to know about him. He had the emotional maturity of a high schooler."

Jack sensed that the incident bothered her more than she was willing to let on. "Can I ask if you know what prompted him to come to the newspaper with the woman?"

Myers was quiet for a moment before admitting, "He was angry with me."

"Why?"

"Because I refused to cancel plans I had one evening to spend time with him."

"Who were your plans with?"

"Steve."

Jack looked at the man in question. He was watching Myers like a hawk, his thumb absently rubbing across the top of her hand. "Was Frank aware of this?"

"He knew."

"Did he know that you two had been previously engaged? I mean I know you had said earlier that nobody knew, but did that include Frank?"

"Frank didn't know. That was something that I never brought up."

"Can I ask why?" Jack asked, wondering why she would have withheld the information if she was seriously involved with Finnegan. Things like that normally were mentioned.

Myers looked at Akard briefly before answering. "I was afraid of what his reaction would be."

Jack frowned at her choice of words. "Did you think he would hurt you?"

"Not physically."

"How about mentally?" Jack asked, knowing that verbal abuse was just as dangerous.

"Maybe. He definitely would have found a way to put a wedge into my relationship with Steve. Frank could be very vindictive when he wanted to be. His bringing that woman into the newspaper that day was nothing compared to what he was capable of."

Jack sat back and finished the remaining coffee in one long swallow. "I appreciate you being so candid. You're being very helpful."

"I want to help. Steve and I both do."

At the mention of Akard's name, Jack looked at the man. "I understand you were covering a political assignment out in the Hamptons yesterday."

"That's right."

"What time did you arrive?"

"I don't know. I left the newspaper around three, so maybe four-thirty or so."

"Is there anybody that can vouch for that? Did you meet with anybody? Talk to anybody?"

Akard's eyes narrowed. "I talked to a lot of people."

"Can you provide the names?"

"Are you asking for an alibi?"

"I'm asking if you can provide the names of anybody who can clear you in this investigation."

Akard was quiet for a brief moment before saying, "I really don't like what you're implying."

"Does that mean you can't give me the information?"

"I can get you the list."

"Can you give it to me now?" Jack asked, not wanting to give him the chance to contact people and ask them to vouch for him.

"I'll give you the list before you leave here. I need some time to compile it."

Jack had a feeling that was going to be his response. "Fair enough. Just out of curiosity though, did Frank say anything to you during your last conversation? Anything that you think might help solve his murder?"

"The last thing Frank told me was to watch my back."

Jack's eyes narrowed. "He threatened you?"

"I didn't take it as that."

"How did you take it?"

"Frank wanted to cover the political fund-raiser. In case you haven't realized it, he was big on covering politics. I just assumed that he was warning me that he was going to somehow get the byline."

"Do you have any idea of why he was so interested in politics?"

"I'm not really sure. There's just something about it that fascinated him."

Jack looked at Myers. "What about you? Did Frank ever talk to you about that particular interest?"

She shook her head. "He never said a word."

Jack contemplated everything he had just learned. "Do either of you have anything else that you'd like to share right now? Anything that you believe might help?"

"No, but if I think of anything I'll let you know. We both will," Myers replied, glancing briefly at Akard while she gave the assurance.

Jack nodded. "You've both been very helpful. And now if you'll excuse me, I'm going to go and check how the search is coming," he said, rising to his feet.

Myers looked up at him. "Do you know how much longer the search will continue for?"

"I'm not sure. Maybe a couple of hours. I'll go and check on the progress, and then I'll be able to give you a better idea."

She started to rise. "I'll come with you."

"I'm afraid I'm going to have to ask you to stay here."

"I won't get in the way."

Jack shook his head slightly. "It would be best if you stayed here. Maybe you can help Steve put together that list for me."

Susan sat back down. "Okay."

The moment Jack walked into the living room, he was struck by how much progress the search team had made. Boxes filled with items were being systematically logged before being carted off, and everything not being taken was put back into its proper place. Jack knew Myers would resent certain items being taken, but he also knew that the team was given strict instructions to only take things that might prove beneficial to the investigation. As he glanced around the room, he caught sight of Ryan by the doorway to the bedroom.

"Hey," Jack greeted as he walked over.

Ryan glanced up. "Hi. Everything okay in there?" he asked, motioning with his head toward the kitchen.

"It was enlightening. I'll fill you in on what I learned later."

"Sounds good."

Jack looked around at the bedroom which was still being searched. "What about you? Did you come across anything?"

Ryan shrugged. "A few things that I believe we can tie to Frank Finnegan personally, but I'm not sure if it'll prove helpful in the case."

"What kind of things?"

"Some personal articles of clothing, a leather binder with some notes."

"Notes?"

"Yeah. They were dated a couple of weeks ago."

"What were they on?"

"Just a local government meeting. They don't mention any names, just the agenda that was covered."

"How much longer do you think this will continue? Susan's getting antsy. I don't want to scare her to the point where she'll totally shut down."

"Understood. I would say in another hour we should be through. We pretty much went through everything already, we're just finishing up some loose ends at this point," Ryan said just as one of the search crew called out to them from the closet.

"What is it?" Ryan asked, watching as the man unearthed a paper bag, buried deep within a box in the closet.

The man carefully pulled a small tape recorder from the bag. "This."

Ryan reached for the electronic device. "It's a little strange to keep a recorder stuffed in a box."

"It's not strange if you're trying to hide it," Jack said as he reached for a pair of latex gloves and quickly donned them. He pressed PLAY and immediately heard a man's voice dictating notes. "That could be Finnegan."

Ryan frowned. "You're not sure?"

"Not positive." He looked at Ryan. "I'm going to go back into the kitchen and see if I can get some more information. Let me know when you're through here."

Chapter Nine

Two hours later, Jack and Ryan were leaving Susan Myers's house. The search team had already packed up and departed, and Steve Akard had given Jack the list of people that he claimed could verify his presence in the Hamptons the day prior, and what time he had arrived.

Ryan motioned to the piece of paper in Jack's hand. "Do you think that the list will check out?"

"I'm sure it will. It's my guess that Akard has already contacted the people he noted and asked them to vouch for his presence. He hesitated too much when I first asked for the list."

"So we'll probably be no closer to the truth."

"I wouldn't say that. Maybe one of the people we talk to who's on Akard's list will prove helpful," Jack said, looking at the list one final time before folding it and putting it in his shirt pocket. "I asked Susan about the recorder."

"And?"

"She admits that it belonged to Finnegan, but she said it's old notes and of no importance. He left it one night, so she just put it in a box for safekeeping. Apparently, he was in no hurry to claim it."

"Do you believe her?"

"I'm not sure. I guess time will tell if she's being truthful," Jack said, glancing at his watch. "Did you want to go and get a bite to eat?"

"I'm a little hungry," Ryan admitted.

"Then why don't we stop for something quick and then head over and talk to Tom Oden. I know he's not working, and from what I gathered from his file when I read through it this morning, he's separated from his wife. He already moved into a different house. Since his career is over and his marriage is on the rocks, I'm hoping that we'll be able to find him at home."

"Stewing in his own misery?"

"Something like that."

"Sounds good to me," Ryan said as he reached for his seatbelt.

"Then let's go," Jack said as he started the car and put it in drive.

An hour later, Jack and Ryan arrived at Tom Oden's house. Situated in an older neighborhood that consisted mainly of bungalows, the small house sat on a tiny lot with overgrown shrubbery, and a lawn that desperately needed to be mowed. Peeling white paint was noticeable on the clapboard, and a few of the shutters were slightly askew, waiting to be fixed.

Jack parked by the curb and peered at the house that looked like it could benefit from the services of a handyman. "Do me a favor and check his file again. I want to be sure that this is the right address. It's not the type of place I expected to find."

Ryan did as Jack requested. "It's the right address. I have to admit though, this isn't the type of house I expected a city official to be living in either."

"Ex-official," Jack reminded him. If outward appearances were any indication, it looked like Oden had fallen on hard times. He recalled the photograph in the man's file of the sprawling ranch that he had previously lived at. This place was a huge departure from that.

"Whatever," Ryan said. "It's still a long way from what I expected."

"Keep in mind that the man is having marital problems. I would imagine that he also has some huge legal fees that he's dealing with."

"Still . . ."

"The important thing to remember is that according to what we were told, Frank Finnegan was responsible for destroying Tom's career as well as his marriage. That alone would indicate that he might have a motive to want the man dead."

"Agreed. Why don't we go and see if he's home," Ryan said, reaching for his door handle.

Jack and Ryan were more than three quarters of the way up the walk when the front door opened to reveal a short, stocky man who appeared to be in his early fifties.

"Can I help you?" the man asked gruffly.

Jack studied the man before him, noticing the unkempt dark-brown hair, wrinkled clothing, and bloodshot eyes. "Tom Oden?"

"Yes?" he responded, squinting his eyes slightly as he tried to bring Jack into focus.

Jack took out his badge and flashed it. "I'm Detective Reeves and this is Detective Parks. We were wondering if we could have a few moments of your time."

"Why?"

"We're investigating the murder of Frank Finnegan."

The man gave a slight start at the mention of the name.

Oden leaned heavily against the doorjamb, causing the wood to creak as it took his full weight. "What does that have to do with me?"

"We understand that you paid a visit to him yesterday."

Though Oden didn't blink at Jack's words, there was a slight tensing of his body. Almost as if he was preparing to fight.

"Mr. Oden?" Jack prompted when the man didn't say anything.

The man's jaw clenched at the mention of his name.

"I have nothing to say that would help you," he said, beginning to close the door.

"We believe you do. If you'd rather do this down at the police station . . ."

"Do I need to call a lawyer?"

"Right now, we just want to talk. But if you would be more comfortable with an attorney . . ."

Oden paused as the implication of Jack's words set in. He studied Jack quietly for a few moments before slowly shaking his head. "No, that's okay. I have nothing to hide." He opened the door fully. "Please come in."

"Thanks," Jack said, as he and Ryan entered the residence. He was relieved that they would be able to talk to the man in his own home. He knew that if Oden had chosen to have his attorney present down at the police station, his answers would have been a lot more guarded.

"Why don't we go into the living room," Oden said, making the offer grudgingly while he motioned with his hand to the right.

"Thanks," Jack said, taking a moment to look over his surroundings. The living room was minimally furnished, containing a couch that he suspected was being used as a bed, a small television set, a TV tray, and two folding lawn chairs.

Oden walked over to the couch and removed the pillow and blanket. "Have a seat," he offered before moving over to one of the lawn chairs. Reaching into his shirt pocket, he took out a pack of cigarettes and a lighter. Pausing briefly, he glanced at Jack and Ryan. "Do you mind if I smoke?"

"Not at all," Jack assured him.

Oden shook out a cigarette and quickly lit it before he took a seat. Reaching down to the floor, he picked up an ashtray and balanced it on the chair's arm. "So tell me, what can I help you with?"

Though the man's voice was normal, Jack didn't miss the slight shaking of his hand as he lit the cigarette. "We'd like to know exactly what your relationship was with Frank Finnegan."

"Relationship?" Oden scoffed. "Frank Finnegan ruined my life. We had no relationship."

"But you do have a lot of animosity," Ryan stated.

"Wouldn't you?"

"We have just one person's point of view on what happened between you two. We were hoping that you could give your side of the story," Jack stated.

Oden grunted. "There's only one story. Frank Finnegan had it in for Drew Kaye, and he didn't care who he took down in his quest to ruin the man."

The bitterness behind the words was not lost on Jack. "Meaning you."

"Meaning me."

"So you think that's the only reason that Frank Finnegan wrote the piece on you? Because you approved the bid submitted by Drew Kaye?"

Oden didn't seem surprised that Jack was aware of

the article Finnegan had wrote. "I know it is. I never had any problem with the guy before that," he replied bitterly.

Jack sensed that the man was being honest. That he hadn't had a prior problem with Finnegan, at least one that had played out in the press. And Jack also had a feeling that if Finnegan was truly set on destroying Kaye, he wouldn't have been concerned with protecting innocent bystanders. He had a ruthless reputation, and he probably would have felt no compunction if someone else ended up getting hurt. "I'm curious. What exactly was Finnegan's problem with Drew Kaye?"

"Drew and Frank went back a long way. They had a lot of history together."

"What kind of history?"

Oden studied Jack quietly for a moment. "They grew up together. They've known each other a long time."

"So how does that translate into Frank Finnegan wanting to do Drew Kaye harm?"

"You're making the assumption that they were friends. They were anything but."

Ryan shifted into a more comfortable position on the sofa. "Can you explain that statement? What makes you think that they weren't friends?"

"If you were ever around the two of them together, you wouldn't even have to ask that question. The tension in the air whenever they were in the same room was always thick."

"Any idea why?"

"No. It's something neither of them ever spoke about. The most I could gather was that it had to do with something that happened when they were in high school."

"Let me take a guess here and say that Drew Kaye has a competitive personality," Jack said, getting a sense of déjà vu.

"I would say that was an accurate assessment."

"If you had to take a guess, what would you say was the cause?" Jack pressed.

Oden's eyebrows lifted. "What's the cause for any rivalry with teenage boys?"

"Teenage girls," Ryan answered.

"Like I said, I don't have any proof, but if I was making a guess . . ."

Jack didn't ask any more on the subject. The man was just speculating, and he needed more than speculation. He needed facts. He knew he would have to get the answers he needed from Kaye. Deciding to redirect the questioning back to the man's visit with Finnegan, he asked, "Why don't you tell us exactly why you went to see Frank Finnegan yesterday."

Oden was quiet for several moments before he expelled a loud sigh. "Look, I may not have liked the man, but I never considered killing him."

"So, why did you feel it was necessary to visit him down at the newspaper?"

"I wanted him to write a retraction. To admit that he sensationalized the story about Drew out of some warped sense of vengeance." Oden took a final drag from his cigarette before grinding the tip into the ashtray.

"And what was his response to that?"

"He just laughed and told me to get lost. According to him, he didn't owe anybody anything. He didn't think he had to rectify anything. He had no remorse, no regret over any of the pain he caused. The man ruined my marriage. He ended my career. Do you think I like living like this? Like an outcast? Everywhere I go, everybody I see knows about that story. They believed his lies. Drew Kaye was awarded the contract to build the new City Hall strictly from his bid amount. There was no favoritism involved. Anybody who bothered to look at the public records would have known that."

"If that's the case, how did Finnegan get away with so many untruths?" Jack asked, curious about the man's response.

"People don't care about truth. They like to see people taken down," Oden replied bitterly. "Even my own wife believed his lies. She couldn't handle the whispers in public places, the humiliation. It was easier for her to just walk away. After twenty years of marriage, she just walked."

"That had to be hard," Jack said, wanting the man to keep talking.

Oden made eye contact with Jack. "What do you want me to say? That I was devastated? That her walking out on me didn't affect me in the least? Well, I won't. If my wife didn't have enough faith in me, then I don't need her in my life."

"You sound very bitter."

Oden gave a humorless laugh. "Bitterness doesn't translate into homicide."

"Nobody said it did," Jack said, more in an effort to calm the man down.

"Don't make me laugh. I know the true reason you're here. I'm a suspect in Frank Finnegan's murder."

"You're a person of interest," Jack corrected. "And you'll remain a person of interest until we can totally clear you. That being said, it would be in your best interest to cooperate."

Oden's jaw clenched, but that was the only indication that they had made an impact. "Is that all?"

"Do you have anything further to say at the moment?"

"I said all I'm going to."

"Fair enough," Jack said, rising to his feet. He reached into his jacket for a business card. "If you want to talk, please call me at this phone number."

Oden reluctantly took the card. "I doubt I'll call you."

Jack nodded. "If that's the case, I can pretty much guarantee that we'll be contacting you. We'll see ourselves out."

"So what did you think?" Ryan asked as they pulled away from the curb.

"The man is hostile."

Ryan gave a humorless laugh. "That's an understatement."

"The question is, did he have enough animosity toward Frank Finnegan to commit murder?"

"We know that given the right circumstances, everybody is capable of it."

"True. It'll be interesting to hear what Drew Kaye has to say."

"Do you think he's going to be willing to talk? We haven't exactly had much luck today in finding people willing to cooperate."

"We won't know until we try." Jack glanced at his watch. "It's early enough where we can still pay Drew Kaye a visit. Let's go talk to the man."

Chapter Ten

It was close to 5:00 when Jack and Ryan arrived at the construction site where Drew Kaye was working. Most of the crew were getting ready to call it a day, and the parking area was busy as the workers were loading up their vehicles in preparation for heading out.

Jack glanced at his watch. "I was hoping that we would be able to catch him before he left for the day."

Ryan motioned to the white pickup parked by a trailer. "It looks like that might be his truck."

Emblazoned on the sides with black lettering was DREW KAYE-CONTRACTOR and a phone number.

They stepped out of their car into the late afternoon sun.

As Jack and Ryan approached the door to the trailer, it

opened, and a blond-haired man with a crew cut stepped out with two other men. He cast a quick, narrow-eyed gaze at Jack and Ryan from behind his wire-framed eyeglasses before turning back to his companions. After several moments of conversation, he waved them off and waited until Jack and Ryan approached.

"Can I help you?" he asked.

"Drew Kaye?"

"Yes?"

Jack took out his badge, flashed it, and made introductions.

Kaye didn't blink. "Why do you want to talk to me?"

"We're investigating Frank Finnegan's murder."

There was a moment of stunned silence before Kaye gave a scoff. "Let me guess. You think I had something to do with that?"

"Did you?" Jack asked, not mincing words. He got the distinct impression that he couldn't afford to where Kaye was concern. The man seemed very controlled, very much aware of how he needed to respond. He couldn't help but wonder if that was because Kaye knew exactly how much importance was going to be placed on his responses.

"Hardly," Kaye again scoffed tersely, but without hesitation.

The curt response wasn't lost on Jack. "Do you have any idea of who would want to see him dead?"

Kaye shrugged. "The man had a lot of enemies."

"Can you help us identify them?"

Kaye studied them silently for a moment, his brown eyes narrowed against the sun. "Why would I help you? I didn't owe Finnegan anything. To the contrary, if the man was alive today, I'd be suing him and that rag of a newspaper he wrote for."

"You sound bitter."

"With good reason."

"Would you care to elaborate?"

"There's no reason to. And like I said, the man had a lot of enemies. You'd be better off investigating one of them."

"We'll be talking to anyone who may have had an issue with the man. But for now . . ."

"But for now I'm it," Kaye said on a sigh. He glanced briefly at his watch. "I have dinner plans tonight."

"We won't take a lot of your time," Jack promised, sensing that the man was trying to find an excuse, any excuse not to talk to them. Jack wasn't willing to let him do that. He sensed that Drew had information that would prove valuable to the investigation, and he was going to do anything in his power to get the man to talk.

When Kaye still hesitated, Jack said, "Of course, we can always meet down at the police station tomorrow first thing."

Kaye hesitated a moment longer before saying, "I guess I can give you a few moments of my time. Let's get out of this heat." He opened the door to the trailer and motioned them inside.

"You may as well have a seat," Kaye offered as he

walked behind a desk to take his own. He took off his eyeglasses and leaned back in his chair. "So tell me what I can help you with."

"We understand you had some problems recently with Frank Finnegan," Jack began.

"I wouldn't exactly say that."

"What would you say?" Ryan asked.

"The man should be sued for libel. He was a careless reporter who didn't care about the truth."

"What do you mean by that?" Jack asked.

"Exactly what the words imply."

Jack suppressed a sigh. He realized that though Kaye had agreed to speak with them, he wasn't going to talk openly or freely. They were going to have to pull the information from him. "Are you stating that the story he wrote when you were awarded the bid to work on City Hall was fabricated?"

Kaye expressed no surprise over the fact that Jack knew what he was referring to. "I am."

"Can you elaborate?"

Kaye went silent again. "I received that bid because my numbers were good. I didn't have a high profit margin on the job, but then that really wasn't my main objective when I submitted the bid."

"What was your objective?"

"In a nutshell, it was to get more bids. I knew that if I did a good job on this project, that I would have a better chance of getting awarded bids for future projects."

"So you decided to low ball the bid?" Ryan asked skeptically.

"I did."

"That seems like a risky thing to do."

"Not really. I considered it smart."

"How? You have bills to pay. It doesn't make sense to not turn a profit," Jack said.

"People remember favors. Things that you do. The next bid I make might not be so advantageous to the city, but they'll remember me and my work. If I'm even close, there's a good chance that I would have been awarded the bid."

"You talk as if it's the past tense."

"It is. Because of Finnegan's story, there's no way I'll be awarded a bid from the city. There'll be too much speculation about possible corruption."

"You make it seem like a foregone conclusion," Ryan said.

Kaye lifted his eyebrow. "Nobody's going to put their career on the line. They saw what happened to Tom Oden."

"We spoke with him today," Jack revealed.

"Did you?"

"He's a very bitter man."

Kaye nodded. "Rightfully so."

Jack watched him closely. "Somehow you don't come across as that. Tell us, did Finnegan's story do as much damage as he had hoped?"

Kaye contemplated Jack for a moment before saying, "You talk as if you know it was intentional."

"Wasn't it?"

"In every sense of the word," Kaye revealed bitterly, giving an indication of just how malicious he thought the piece to be. "Frank and I go way back."

"So we understand."

Kaye looked at Jack curiously. "Who have you been talking to?"

"Does it matter?"

"It might. But let me take a guess here and say that Tom Oden gave you a rundown on Frank's and my history."

"He mentioned something."

"He told you that Frank and I grew up together."

"He did," Jack said, not bothering to hide the knowledge.

"That doesn't surprise me."

"Why's that?"

"Because Tom blames me in part for his trouble."

"Why?" Ryan asked.

"He thinks that Frank Finnegan wrote the article to get back at me. He considers himself just an innocent bystander who got caught in the crossfire."

"Get back at you for what?" Jack asked curiously.

"For dating Susan Myers."

"Susan Myers? The same woman that works at *The Chronicle*?"

"Yes. I took her to dinner one night and Frank found

out about it. I guess you could say that it brought back old memories."

"How long ago did you take her out?" Jack asked.

"Maybe three weeks ago."

Jack pondered. "When you mentioned that you thought it brought back old memories, exactly what were you referring to?"

Kaye didn't respond.

"Mr. Kaye, we're not asking for the sake of prying. What you say might help us with Frank Finnegan's murder investigation."

Kaye was quiet for a moment before nodding. "Frank and I grew up together. We went to the same schools. Elementary, junior high, and high school. Frank always seemed to think he was better than everybody else. When Frank was seeing one of the cheerleaders in high school, I kind of took it as a challenge to see if I could take her away from him." He paused for a moment before saying, "It was immature, but harmless."

"Frank didn't see it that way," Jack guessed.

Kaye slowly shook his head and reached for a pack of cigarettes on his desk. Shaking one from the pack, he lit the tip before responding. "Hardly. Especially when I succeeded."

"You don't sound like you regret it," Ryan said.

"I was young and foolish. Taking her away from Frank did great things for my ego. But Frank never forgave me. Things have been tense between us ever since."

"Is that why you took Susan Myers out? To irritate Frank?" Jack asked.

Kaye gave a shrug and took another drag from his cigarette. "It was a benefit."

Jack didn't like the vague answer. Experience had taught him that people resorted to that tactic when they had something to hide. "Is that a yes?"

"Maybe in part."

"Meaning?"

"Meaning I kind of liked getting at Frank. Don't get me wrong. I enjoyed Susan's company immensely, but I also liked getting under Frank's skin."

Jack couldn't fault the man for being honest. "Do you think that's why he wrote the article?"

"I know it was."

"Why are you so sure?"

"Because Frank was a very jealous individual."

Jack didn't miss the way the man had no trouble talking about the man in the past tense. He found it interesting. Most people didn't talk about murder victims in the past tense, especially when it was such a recent occurrence. "So?"

"I'm quite sure that the article he wrote was his way of getting even."

"With you."

"With me."

"And what about Susan?"

"What about her?"

"Would Frank have done anything to her in retaliation?" Jack asked.

"Are you asking if he would have hurt her?"

"Yes."

"Not physically."

"But emotionally?"

"He was more than capable of that."

"Did you have contact with Susan after that night?"

"No."

"Not even by phone?"

"No. Why?"

"Just curious if she had mentioned anything about Frank Finnegan's reaction to her going out with you."

"I'm afraid I can't help you with that. While I enjoyed Susan's company that night, we both realized that there was no future for us."

Jack was quiet for a moment. "Did you have any reason to want to see Finnegan dead?"

Kaye looked stunned but he quickly recovered his wits. "I didn't kill him if that's what you're asking."

"Do you know of anybody who would have wanted to see him dead?"

"Metaphorically, there were a lot of people who wished Frank harm. He wasn't an easy person to get along with under the best of circumstances, and he rubbed a lot of people the wrong way. But I honestly can't think of anybody who would have actually had the guts to commit the crime."

"I just have one more question if you don't mind."

"What?"

"From my understanding, Frank Finnegan liked covering political news stories. Since you grew up with him, I was wondering if you would have any idea of why."

"You want to know why he had an interest in politics?"

"I'm curious."

Kaye shrugged. "I assume it's because his father was involved in politics. He probably just had a natural interest."

"Local politics?"

"Yeah. Frank's father had grand ambitions. I think his goal was to make it to Congress."

"I take it by that statement that he didn't obtain his goal?"

"No, he didn't."

"What happened?"

"He had a heart attack when he was forty-three. It was fatal."

"That's rough."

"Yeah, it is."

Jack waited several moments to see if the man would say anything else, but when it became apparent that he wasn't going to he reached for one of his cards. "You've been very helpful. We appreciate the time you took in talking to us. Here's my card. If you can think of anything that you think may be helpful with this investigation, please call."

Kaye hesitated for several moments before he reached for the card. He glanced at it briefly. "Of course."

Jack sensed that the man wouldn't be calling them. The words were just meant to placate. "Then if there's nothing else that you'd care to say at the moment, we'll be heading out."

Kaye nodded. "Contrary to any impression I might have given you, I never wanted to see Frank dead."

Jack didn't respond to the statement. There was nothing to say. "We'll see ourselves out."

The moment Jack and Ryan were outside, Ryan spoke. "So what do you think of Drew Kaye?"

"He seemed very calm. Very collected. Maybe too much so."

"You think he's hiding something?"

"I think it's more than a possibility. We'll have to see what else we can dig up on him." Jack looked at his watch. "Let's see what we can learn about Lisa Reyes and then touch base with Ed before we call it a day."

Chapter Eleven

Ashley was lying on the sofa watching television with John when Jack walked into the house. She looked up as he walked through the door, and held a finger against her lips while she motioned down to their young son, who was on the verge of falling asleep.

Jack smiled slightly at the picture his son made, laying peacefully against Ashley, his little fist entangled in her blond hair, his eyelids in the last stage of fluttering while he fought to stay awake. Knowing that any distraction would have him sitting up, Jack carefully closed the door. Shrugging out of his suit jacket, he hung it on the hallway closet doorknob. He waited a minute while his son succumbed fully to sleep before walking further into the living room.

Ashley smiled slightly at Jack's careful approach. John was over-tired and had fought taking a nap that afternoon, so she knew if Jack woke him that it would be a chore to get him back down. Still rubbing the toddler's back, she whispered to Jack, "Can you take John up to bed?"

"Yeah," Jack whispered back, reaching down and picking him up. "I'll be back in a few."

Jack took John upstairs and carefully laid him in his toddler bed. He stood there for several moments, rubbing his son's back soothingly while he settled into sleep. Satisfied that he wouldn't wake up, Jack carefully backed out of the room, keeping the bedroom door open halfway so that he and Ashley could hear him if he awoke.

Walking down the stairs, Jack heard Ashley moving around in the kitchen, and he made his way to the room. "He's out like a light."

Ashley turned when she heard him enter, a smile hovering on her lips. "Good. He had a busy day."

"Me too."

"I missed you today."

Jack walked over to kiss her. "I missed you too."

Ashley returned the kiss and melted in his embrace. "Are you hungry? I saved some dinner for you."

"I'm starving."

"Then why don't you sit down and relax. It will only take a couple of minutes to get it heated."

"You don't have to do that. I'll take care of it."

"Nonsense. Relax."

"Thanks," Jack said, reaching up and loosening his tie. He pulled a chair out from under the table with his foot before taking a seat.

Ashley looked over at him sympathetically, noticing how tired he looked, imagining how tired he felt. Jack gave one hundred percent of himself to a case, and she knew he had been on overload for the last two days. Taking the plate she had saved him out of the refrigerator, she walked over to the microwave. "Rough day?"

Jack ran a weary hand across the back of his neck. "Busy," he corrected.

"Did you find out anything that will help with the investigation?" she asked, removing the plastic wrap from the plate and popping it into the microwave before setting the timer.

"We found out a lot of stuff, but it'll take some time to piece everything together and see where it takes us."

"Did you get a chance to talk to Susan again?"

"Yeah. Why?"

"No reason. I was speaking to one of my friends down at the paper and they said she requested a leave of absence. I thought maybe she was planning on leaving town."

"Why would you think that?" Jack asked, surprised by the news. Though when he thought about it, he supposed it wasn't that strange. Especially considering the relationship she had with Finnegan.

"Because Steve Akard requested a leave also."

Ashley's words caught Jack short. "Are you sure?"

he asked, thinking that put a different spin on things. Especially considering the relationship between the two of them. He could see Myers taking some time off, but not Akard. The man didn't seem upset about Finnegan's death, and he and Myers supposedly hadn't had a romantic type of relationship for years. He suddenly wondered if Akard's feelings for Myers were deeper than either of them let on. If he could have been jealous of her involvement with Finnegan.

"Yeah."

"That's strange."

"Why?"

"Because we spoke with both of them today and neither one of them mentioned anything."

"Really," Ashley said, contemplating Jack's response while she took the plate of food out of the microwave and brought it over to the table.

"Really," Jack said before looking down at the pot roast, potatoes and carrots laid before him. "Looks good," he said in appreciation.

"Tastes better," she quipped, walking back to the refrigerator and removing a pitcher of iced tea. Reaching for a glass in the cupboard, she poured Jack a glass.

"Thanks."

"You're welcome," she replied before changing the topic of conversation back to Finnegan's murder investigation. "Who else did you talk to today besides Susan and Steve?"

"Tom Oden. Drew Kaye."

"That's interesting."

Jack looked at her, "Why do you say that?"

"No reason. I can just imagine what they had to say after the piece Frank had written," she said, familiar with the article.

"Yeah, well, I would definitely say there was no love lost."

"Did they say anything that was helpful?"

"Quite a bit actually. But the most interesting thing that was said revolved around Susan Myers."

"Susan?"

Jack took a sip of his iced tea. "Apparently Drew Kaye dated her."

Ashley shook her head slightly in confusion. "But I thought she was dating Frank Finnegan."

"She was. But according to Drew, he also took her out."

"How long ago?"

"Maybe three weeks ago," Jack said while taking a bite of the pot roast.

"Which might have been what caused Frank to parade the other woman in front of Susan," Ashley said.

"It's possible."

"Did Susan mention any of this to you?"

Jack shook his head. "Not a word."

"Interesting," Ashley murmured.

"Yes it is. And unfortunately, it still leaves a lot of unanswered questions. Because we also found out that Lisa Reyes, the woman Frank was with last week, is out of the country attending a friend's wedding. She's devastated by the news, and swears she has no idea of who may have wanted Finnegan dead."

"When did she leave?"

"Two days ago."

Ashley was quiet before asking, "How can I help you find the answers?"

"Unless you have some way to get Susan to talk, I don't know if you can."

"I can try."

"I doubt if you'll have any success. She knows I'm your husband. My guess is she's not going to open up."

"We won't know until I try."

Jack looked at her curiously. "And how do you plan on doing that?"

"I'll call her up and ask her to lunch."

"What makes you think she'll go? As far as I can recall, you haven't invited her to lunch before. She'll know you'll have an ulterior motive."

"Maybe. But my guess is that she'll be so curious about what I have to say, she won't be able to say no. She knows she's a person of interest. If she thinks that I might be able to give her some idea about just how much suspicion she's under, she'll be more than willing to meet with me."

Jack contemplated. "It might work."

"There's no might about it. Susan may just be an administrative assistant, but she works for a newspaper. Curiosity is part of her job."

Jack hated involving Ashley, but he knew she may be able to succeed in getting the answers. After a long pause, he said, "As long as you're careful . . ."

"I'll be very discreet."

"You can't make her feel threatened," he warned, knowing that Ashley could come on like a ton of bricks when she wanted. She was tenacious as a reporter, and he knew that was a natural part of who she was.

"She won't."

"I don't know," he said, still hesitating.

"Come on, Jack. You know you have nothing to lose."

"Susan might be dangerous. If she's the one that killed Frank Finnegan . . ."

"If she was, she did it because Frank hurt her and her emotions were involved. I don't think she would prove a threat to me."

Jack hesitated a moment longer. "All right."

"Great," Ashley said, not giving him a chance to change his mind. "I'll call her first thing tomorrow and arrange to meet."

"I'm still not sure if this is the right way to go about this."

"It'll be fine, Jack. Don't worry."

"Famous last words."

"I'll be careful."

"You call me the minute you learn something. If she slips and even hints that she had something to do with Finnegan's death, I want you out of there."

"Agreed."

Jack ran a hand through his hair. "And if Akard is there . . ."

"The meeting won't take place."

"Okay."

"Relax, Jack. If it makes you feel any better, I'll ask some of the other girls down at the newspaper to have lunch with us also. It might put Susan more at ease."

"It might."

"I'll start calling people in the morning to see if I can get two others to meet with us."

"Be sure that nobody knows what you're up to."

"You can count on me."

Jack smiled. "I know I can."

Ashley smiled and reached for the pitcher of iced tea and refilled his glass. "Finish eating."

"I will."

"You want to know what John did today?" Ashley asked, knowing her husband often missed their son's milestones.

"I would love to know what he did," Jack assured her, his face softening at the mention of John.

"He learned to lock and unlock the door."

Jack froze. "Which room?"

"His bedroom. I mean I didn't panic or anything, especially since we put the keys above the doorframes, but it gave me a few moments of pause."

"I can imagine."

"And of course John thought it was one big game. He was laughing the entire time."

"I hope you explained to him the dangers of doing that. I mean at our house we can get into the rooms, but if we were visiting someone . . ."

"I know. I'll keep reinforcing to him that he can't do it."

"He's getting so big," Jack said, putting down his flatware.

"Yeah, he is," she said, looking down at his clean plate. "Did you have enough to eat?"

"Plenty. It was delicious by the way."

"Thank you. Did you want dessert?"

"What do we have?"

"Apple pie?"

Jack thought about it. "Sounds good, but I'd better not," he said, getting up from his chair and rinsing his plate before placing it in the dishwasher. "Morning comes very quickly these days."

"Are you ready to turn in?" Ashley asked, rising from the table to put away the iced tea.

Jack wiped down the wooden table before throwing the sponge in the sink. "I am," he said, holding out his hand to her. "Shall we?"

Ashley put her hand in his. "I don't think that I told you today that I love you."

Jack smiled down at her. "The feeling's mutual."

"We're very lucky."

"Yes, we are," he agreed, squeezing her hand slightly. "Come on. Let's go to bed."

Chapter Twelve

Jack was sound asleep when the phone rang at 5:00 the next morning. He awoke with a start, squinted at the clock, and reached for the receiver. "Hello," he answered, his voice raspy from sleep.

"Jack?"

Jack recognized Ed's voice immediately, and he was instantly wide awake. Ed would only call if there was an emergency or a break in a case. "Ed, what's up?" he asked, sitting up in bed.

"I'm sorry to call so early, but I need you to get to Frank Finnegan's house."

"Why? What's going on?"

"There was a break-in."

Jack stiffened. "How long ago?"

"Maybe an hour or so. A neighbor was walking his dog and he noticed a light in one of the rooms."

"Did Finnegan have a timer set?"

"None that was noted when we did the initial search. The neighbor thought it was the beam from a flashlight. We sent a squad car out, but whoever was there had already gone."

Jack ran a weary hand through his hair. "Did the patrolmen find the point of entry?"

"The sliding glass door in the back of the house. There was no security bar in place. It was relatively easy for whoever it was to gain access."

"Was the glass on the door broken?"

"No, it wasn't even scratched."

"What about Frank Finnegan's personal belongings. Do we know if they got anything?"

Ed let out an audible sigh. "Unfortunately, we're not sure as of yet. And to be honest, I don't know if we'll ever have that answer. There's nobody to give us a list of inventory."

"What about the search team? Didn't they create an inventory list when they searched the place? Something we could use for comparison purposes?" Jack asked, knowing that it was usually standard procedure.

"They just noted what they took. I know it was handled a little differently than our normal procedure, but keep in mind that there were no relatives to sign off on it."

"So we can't be sure if this was a random break-in or if it has something to do with Finnegan's murder."

"That's right. Which is why we have to treat it as if it were the latter." Ed paused. "How long do you think it will take you to get there?"

"Give me about half an hour."

"You got it. I'll call Ryan and we'll both meet you there."

"I'll see you in a bit."

"What happened?" Ashley murmured, having heard Jack's part of the conversation.

Jack turned and met her eyes through the darkness. He hated leaving her, he hated the fact that he wouldn't have time to spend with John in the morning, but duty called. He reached out and caressed her cheek with the back of his hand. "Frank Finnegan's house was broken into. I have to go," he said, swinging out of bed.

Ashley watched him walk over to the closet. "Jack?"

"Yeah?"

"Be careful."

He gave her a slight smile. "I always am. Try and get some sleep. John will be up soon enough," he said before going into the bathroom and closing the door so that he could get ready without disturbing Ashley.

Ed and Ryan were already on site as Jack pulled up to Finnegan's house. Several squad cars were parked by the curb, and a steady stream of police personnel were entering and leaving the residence as they conducted a search.

After parking his car, Jack made his way over to the

two men. "Hey. I hope you two haven't been waiting long."

"Hi," Ed replied, turning at the sound of Jack's voice. "We just got here a few minutes ago ourselves. By the way, I'm sorry about the early call. I hope I didn't wake the rest of the family."

"Just Ashley. But don't worry. She should be able to fall back to sleep. She's used to getting up with John."

"Regardless, give her my apologies when you see her."

"I will," Jack assured him before motioning to the house and its activity. "Did you go in yet?"

"No, we were just getting briefed by the first officer on the scene. He had the chance to interview the neighbor who reported the break-in."

"And?"

"Other than seeing the light, the guy couldn't tell us much. He didn't see any strangers hanging around earlier."

"Then I guess we'd better get in there and see what we're dealing with," Jack said, turning to lead the way.

The interior was in total chaos, and a soft whistle escaped from Jack's lips as he surveyed the drawers that were emptied, the closet contents that were strewn about, and the cushions of the sofa that had been ripped with a knife and the stuffing pulled out in clumps.

"It looks like somebody was looking for something," Jack said.

Ed walked further into the room, surveying the damage. "The questions is, what?"

Ryan reached for a pair of latex gloves on one of the evidence cases and quickly donned them before bending down to pick up some of the foam torn from the sofa. "What could you hide in a sofa?"

"It's anybody's guess. Frank was a reporter and his files are his livelihood. It would make sense that maybe he had something on someone and used the inside of the cushion as a hiding place," Jack said.

"You think they were looking for a file?" Ed asked.

"Maybe."

Ed cast him a quick glance. "Digital or paper?"

"Digital. Maybe a portable USB stick. It's a small enough device where he could find any number of places to hide it, and they have a large storage capacity."

Ryan looked at him curiously. "You think Frank had information on the person who murdered him?"

Jack swept a hand around the room. "Based on this break-in, I don't think we can discount it."

"The break-in could have been done by someone who knows Frank Finnegan's dead. They might have seen the empty house as an open invitation. Especially knowing that the owner wouldn't be returning home," Ryan suggested.

"Possibly," Jack agreed.

"Regardless, if the person that broke in was the same person who killed Finnegan, he or she might have had a different motive than just revenge," Ed said. "Maybe Finnegan had something on them that they couldn't afford to have made public."

"I can't argue that. It's definitely a consideration," Jack said.

Ed grunted. "Hopefully whoever broke in was careless and left some fingerprints or DNA."

Jack put on latex gloves and walked over to the desk that had been ransacked. He began sorting through the items on the floor, being careful not to compromise any evidence. As he moved a paperweight out of the way, he noticed the glitter of a small diamond solitaire earring on the floor.

Jack reached for a pen and evidence bag, and carefully maneuvered the piece of jewelry into the bag before sealing it. Picking up the small stud, he studied it. There was nothing fancy or ostentatious about the earring. It was a simple solitaire. He knew it could belong to either a man or a woman, and he tried to recall if Finnegan had a pierced ear. Though he never recalled seeing the man wear an earring when he had run into him at the newspaper back when Ashley worked there, he knew a lot of men wouldn't necessarily wear the piece of jewelry in a business setting, especially if they worked around conservative people.

"What did you find?" Ryan asked.

"An earring."

Ryan frowned and walked closer. "Do you think it belongs to a woman?"

"It's a small diamond stud. It could belong to either a man or a woman." Jack paused then asked Ed, "Do we know if Frank Finnegan had a pierced ear?"

"He didn't," Ed replied.

"Are you sure?"

"Positive. I got a copy of his autopsy report yesterday while you two were making rounds. There were no piercings."

"It could be that the earring belongs to Susan," Ryan suggested. "I mean she was seeing the guy . . ."

"True," Ed said. "But the question is, did she leave it at the house when Frank was alive, or after the break-in?"

Jack looked at Ed. "Would the search team you had sent to the house the night Finnegan was murdered have overlooked the earring?"

"It would have been careless, but it's possible," Ed acknowledged. "Especially since it wasn't something that they would have been looking for."

"Maybe we'll get lucky and we'll be able to pick up a partial print off the stone. If not, there should definitely be DNA on it."

"Considering the size of the earring, lifting any type of print is going to be a long shot," Ryan pointed out.

Jack grunted. "True, but right now we don't have much else to go on."

"I took the liberty of sending out a few patrol cars. They're going to ride by our people of interest and see if there's anything that catches their attention. They'll let me know if anything surfaces," Ed said.

Just then there was a shout from the back door.

The three of them walked over to the sliding glass

door, pushing past several technicians that were gathered by the opening.

"What is it?" Jack asked, watching as a crime scene investigator was carefully lifting a black object off the ground. Frowning, Jack moved closer until he recognized the item as a black ski mask.

"Where did you find it?" Jack asked.

"In the bush next to the door," the technician responded.

Jack grabbed a flashlight and went over to the bush. Shining the item on the ground, he paused as he caught a slight reflection. "I need an evidence bag," he called out.

Ed walked closer. "What did you find?"

Jack looked up. "It looks like the clasp to the earring we found inside," he said, studying the object. The small gold butterfly clasp looked like an exact match to the earring discovered inside, and he instinctively knew that the earring had been worn by the intruder that evening. And while common sense indicated it was a female who was in the residence, pinpointing Susan Myers as the main suspect, he couldn't overlook the fact that many men wore earrings also.

Thinking back, he tried to recall if he saw a piercing on Steve Akard, Tom Oden, or Drew Kaye. His observation skills were usually pretty good, and he didn't recall seeing any glitter on the three men.

"What are you thinking about?"

"If Steve Akard, Tom Oden, or Drew Kaye had been wearing an earring when we visited them yesterday."

"They weren't," Ryan replied.

"Are you sure?"

"Positive. But I can tell you that Susan has pierced ears."

"Yeah, I know. But she was wearing small hoops when we talked to her."

"So? Women change earrings all the time. Jane has been known to change hers three times a day, depending on what we're doing."

Jack grunted. "Ashley has changed hers a couple of times during the day too," he recalled just as Ed's cell phone rang.

"Stall." Ed was quiet while the caller spoke, and then he ended the call.

"Who was that?" Jack asked, wondering if the call had something to do with the patrol cars that Ed had sent out.

Ed expelled a harsh sigh. "There were lights on at Susan Myers's house, as well as Tom Oden's."

"What about Drew Kaye and Steve Akard?"

"Kaye's place was quiet, but there was a man at Susan's. The patrolman noticed him through the window."

"Meaning Akard," Jack said.

"It's definitely a possibility."

"We should be able to pick up some DNA off the back of the earring post. It may help us nail the person responsible for Finnegan's murder because I seriously doubt that whoever broke in here tonight did it for no reason. Whoever came here tonight was looking for something. Something that's going to tie them to the murder."

Ryan stuck his hands in his pockets and rocked back on his heels. "So how do you want to proceed?"

Jack handed the small bag containing the gold clasp to one of the technicians to be cataloged. "Right now, I'd like to start applying a little more pressure to all of our suspects. We won't be able to get the DNA results from this earring right away, but our killer may not know that. If we apply some pressure, we may be able to get the break we need to solve this case."

Chapter Thirteen

It was almost nine in the morning by the time Jack and Ryan arrived at Susan Myers's apartment. The search team was still back at Finnegan's house securing the residence, and Ed had decided to head back to the office to see if any new information came in on the suspects while Jack and Ryan decided to pay a surprise visit to Myers, hoping they would be able to find out exactly why she was up so early that morning, and whether or not it had anything to do with the break-in.

As Jack parked the car, he took a few moments to glance around. Most of the parking spots were empty, and Jack concluded that the majority of residents were probably at work. Looking at the bay window of Myers's apartment, Jack noticed that both her windows and blinds were closed.

Jack glanced at Ryan. "She's either still sleeping or she's not home."

"Let's hope that it's the former," Ryan said as he unbuckled his seatbelt.

Jack grunted in agreement. "I guess if she was the one who was at Finnegan's this morning, it would stand to reason that she might be exhausted from her early morning trek." He raked fingers through his hair before reaching up and adjusting the knot of his tie. "Are you ready?"

"As ready as I'll ever be."

"Then come on, let's go."

The apartment was quiet as they walked up to the door, with only the steady hum of the air conditioner filling the air.

Jack glanced at Ryan before he reached out and pressed the doorbell. Waiting patiently, he tried to detect the sound of footsteps from within the apartment but he heard nothing. After a full minute passed with no answer, he pressed the doorbell again.

There was more silence before he heard footsteps coming to the door, but it was a few seconds longer before the knob turned and the door was pulled open to reveal Susan Myers.

"Good morning, Susan," Jack greeted, hoping the informal greeting would help in keeping her suspicions from being raised. He looked at her from behind his sunglasses, noticing that she looked as if she had literally just awoke. She wore a short cotton robe that fell to her knees, and her eyes were red-rimmed from lack of sleep. But it was her hair that suggested she had just risen from bed. The hair that she normally wore like a curtain around her face was tousled and standing on end. She looked different than when he had seen her previously— more vulnerable, and Jack was suddenly glad that they decided to seek her out. He knew that her defenses weren't in play. They stood a good chance of getting honest answers from her.

Myers squinted as she stared at them and stifled a yawn behind one manicured hand. "Detectives. Is something wrong?"

"No," Jack responded, immediately noticing that her nail polish was chipped on some of her fingers. And while he knew that housework alone could have caused it, he couldn't help but wonder if it had been done while breaking into Finnegan's home. "We just need a few moments of your time."

She looked at him curiously. "It's kind of early . . ."

Jack glanced briefly at his watch. "It's nine o'clock. I'm sorry if I woke you . . ."

Her eyes met his. "Is it? I guess I didn't sleep well last night. I feel like I just went to bed." She hid another yawn behind her hand while she opened the door a little wider. "Please, come in," she said, stepping back.

She ran a weary hand through her hair, pushing some strands away from her face. As she did, Jack noticed that she had on only one earring. A gold diamond solitaire stud. The image of the earring uncovered at Finnegan's house flashed through his mind. "I hope we're not disturbing you, but it's important that we speak with you."

"Important?" she repeated, her eyes widening slightly.

"It's about Frank Finnegan."

Myers closed her eyes briefly. "Of course. You'll have to excuse me. To be honest, I was sound asleep when you rang the bell. I'm taking a few days off from work while I try and deal with Frank's death, and I've been exhausted," she admitted softly.

"That's understandable."

Myers hid another yawn behind her hand. "Sorry. I'm never my best before coffee."

"We can talk while you're getting your coffee."

"Okay," she said, pausing for a quick moment before asking, "Would you like a cup?"

Jack smiled slightly. "That would be great."

She nodded. "Then let's go into the kitchen."

As they walked through to the kitchen, Jack took note of the apartment. Everything that the search crew had moved the previous day had been put back into its place. And considering that the crew had been extremely careful to make sure the search had been as painless as possible, Jack thought it was interesting that Myers wasted no time in reorganizing the place. It showed that she paid careful attention to details.

As they entered the kitchen, she motioned to the kitchen table. "Please, take a seat."

"Thanks," Jack murmured, sitting down with Ryan.

Myers glanced over her shoulder while she filled the

glass carafe from the coffeepot with cold water at the sink. "So tell me, what brings you here? You mentioned that you had some additional questions and that it was about Frank. Did you find anything that might tell you who killed him?"

"We're not sure."

Myers shot Jack a sharp look. "What do you mean?" she asked, while turning off the water and moving over to the automatic coffeepot to put the water in the reservoir and add the filter and coffee grinds.

"Frank's house was broken into this morning."

Myers stilled. "It was broken into?"

"Yes," Jack said, noticing that she had paled slightly.

"That's terrible!"

"It is."

She leaned back against the counter while she looked at him. "What exactly does that have to do with me?"

"We were wondering if you went out early this morning?"

"Why do you ask?"

"Since there was a break-in at Finnegan's house, we need to know your whereabouts this morning. Around four o'clock specifically."

"Why?" she asked, paling slightly.

Jack suddenly sensed that she wasn't going to talk to them willingly. "We need to know if you had anything to do with it."

Total silence followed his statement. "What?" she asked after a full minute.

"We need to know where you were this morning around four o'clock," Jack repeated.

"I was here," she said after several moments, her breath catching slightly as if she was gasping for air.

"You didn't leave the house at all?"

"No."

When she didn't expand any further, Jack said, "We know you were awake at around six fifteen." He watched as she tensed.

She stared at him with wide eyes. "How do you know that?"

"A patrol car drove by."

There was a moment of stunned silence before she said, "You honestly think I had something to do with the break-in."

Jack didn't respond to her charge. Instead he said, "They noticed that a man was with you."

Myers seemed shocked that she had been under such scrutiny, and she closed her eyes briefly before slowly leaning back against the counter. "It was Steve."

"Steve Akard?"

"Yes."

"He came by at that hour?" Jack asked, wondering if the person that they should actually be talking to was Akard.

Myers shook her head. "No. He was here until that hour. After you and your search team left yesterday, Steve stayed with me."

"He never left?"

"No."

Jack considered the relevancy of her statement. "I thought you said that you were just friends."

"We are. Which is why he stayed."

"I'm not quite following you . . ." Jack needed to know if she was trying to use Akard as an alibi, and if Akard would try to do the same by admitting that he had stayed with Myers. Jack knew that based on her remarks, he and Ryan would be talking to Akard later that day.

Myers ran a shaky hand through her hair. "Steve knew that the search that was done here totally threw me. He stayed to provide moral support and fell asleep on the sofa. He was here until about seven this morning."

"Why did he leave at seven?"

"He had to be at work this morning, so he left to shower and change. When your patrol officer drove by this morning, he probably saw Steve and I sharing a cup of coffee before he left to go back to his place."

"So neither of you left your place in the early morning hours?" Jack pressed, trying to see if there were any inconsistencies in her answers.

"No. We didn't. Can I ask you something?"

"Of course."

She hesitated only a moment before asking, "Why would you think that one of us had something to do with the break-in?"

"We're just taking precautions," Jack replied, not wanting to mention anything about the earring being found.

"Are you sure that's all? I mean I don't have a lot of experience with the law, but it seems a little strange that I'm being singled out."

"I suppose it does. But since you had a relationship with Frank Finnegan, it stands to reason that you could offer a lot to the case. You could supply information that might help us solve his murder."

"But you thought that I might have broken into his house . . ."

"We have to rule it out. If you had gone to Finnegan's house, it's possible you would have only gone to retrieve some personal items," Jack said, giving her the opening to make an admission if she felt the need to, and being careful to keep any hint of accusation from his voice.

She stared at Jack quietly for a moment. "I didn't go to Frank's house," she said, turning back to the coffee.

Jack couldn't help but notice that her hand was less than steady. "You had mentioned that Steve had to be at work today."

"That's right," she replied without turning around. "He had planned to take some time off to spend with me, but unfortunately duty called. With Frank gone, there's a lot of loose ends. He had a meeting with the editor first thing this morning."

"Any idea about what?"

Myers was quiet for a moment before admitting, "Somebody has to cover the stories that Frank was working on."

"And that someone is Steve Akard."

"It makes sense. Steve is familiar with all the stories that had been assigned to Frank. It will be easy enough for him to fill in any blanks."

Her words had Jack looking at her curiously. "You had mentioned the two of them had always been in competition with each other."

Myers brought the coffee to the table. "So?"

"So doesn't that mean that Steve will be benefiting somehow from Finnegan's death?"

She gave him a sharp look. "Steve might have been in competition with Frank, but that doesn't mean he wanted him dead."

"But he would have had a lot to gain."

"You're referring to Frank's assignments?"

"Yes."

Myers immediately shook her head. "Steve's a good reporter. He wouldn't have to resort to murder to get stories."

Jack took a sip of his coffee. "About what time did you get to sleep last night?" he asked, trying to put together some sort of time line.

"Maybe midnight."

"And Steve?"

"He fell asleep on the couch about eleven."

"And you went straight to bed? You didn't leave the apartment for anything?"

"No, I didn't. My neighbor can vouch for that."

Jack gave her a sharp look. "What do you mean?"

Myers gave a slight shrug. "Steve and I were going to run out and get a bite to eat about eight last night, except my car wouldn't start due to a dead battery. My neighbor tried to jump it since he was parked right next to me, but it didn't work. I need to arrange to have my car towed this morning to a service station."

"What about Steve's car?"

"What about it?"

"I'm assuming it was running?"

"Yes."

"So why didn't he drive to the restaurant?"

"To be honest, he wanted to. I think he would have done almost anything to get out of the apartment for a little while."

"But?"

"But I was so aggravated by what happened to my car that we decided to just stay home. We made a frozen pizza and watched a movie."

"So you didn't go out at all?"

"No," she said just as she reached up to push her hair behind her ears. The moment her fingers glided over her earlobes, she paused.

"What's the matter?"

Myers fingered one of her lobes. "I just realized I lost one of my earrings."

"When did you see it last?"

"I put them on last night before we attempted to go out to dinner," she said, pushing her chair back from the table and looking around the floor.

Jack noticed that she seemed extremely agitated. He couldn't help but wonder if it was due to the fact that she was realizing that she might have dropped the earring at a crime scene. "I take it they're valuable."

"They're priceless to me. They were my last gift from Frank," she told him before rising from her chair. "Would you excuse me for a moment?"

"Of course," Jack said, as she quickly left the room.

"What do you think?" Ryan asked the moment she was gone.

Jack took another sip. "She seems very concerned that the earring has been lost. The question is, just how much is this going to throw her?" They heard the sound of a thump from the other room.

Several minutes passed before Myers returned to the kitchen. Though her face was slightly pale, she didn't look like she was in a full-fledged panic anymore.

"Is everything okay?" Jack asked.

She gave a slight nod. "It is now."

"You found what you were looking for?"

She nodded and held out a hand, revealing her missing earring. "My earring was stuck to my pillow on the bed."

Chapter Fourteen

"What's your impression?" Ryan asked the moment they were back in the car and the air conditioner was on full blast.

Jack sighed and ran a weary hand over his head. "I'm not sure. I thought that we were going to be able to prove that she was the one who broke into Finnegan's house this morning. That was until she found the earring in her bedroom."

"I thought so too. It definitely looked like a match to the one found at Finnegan's. But since it's not, that leaves us with two possible new theories. Either there's another woman involved, or one of the male suspects has a pierced ear."

"If we follow the train of thought that the person who broke into Finnegan's house was also the person responsible for murdering him, the killer would have to be a man. We don't have another woman that we can place at the newspaper on the evening Finnegan was killed that had an issue with the guy."

"It's entirely possible the break-in had nothing to do with the murder," Ryan reminded him.

Jack shot him a look of disbelief. "Do you really think that's likely based on the way the house was trashed?"

"It's a possibility."

"I seriously doubt that anyone would have gone to the trouble of ripping up a sofa cushion unless they were looking for something specific. The scene at Finnegan's place didn't indicate a random break-in."

"Kids can be vandals," Ryan reminded him.

"True. And I have no doubt that if it had been kids that they would have no compunction about doing as much damage as possible. But the rest of the house wasn't trashed in a way that indicated that. Whoever broke in was looking for something specific."

"It did appear that way."

"So considering everything, unless we can tie another motive into the break-in, I think we have to go on the assumption that the break-in and the murder are somehow tied together."

Ryan was quiet for a moment before asking, "So where do we go from here?"

"Susan mentioned that Steve Akard left this morning because he was going to be covering some of the stories that had originally been assigned to Finnegan."

"So?"

"So, even though Susan admits that he spent the evening at her place sleeping on the couch, it's not a solid alibi. He could have easily left the apartment after she had gone to bed. Depending on how sound of a sleeper she is, she may not have heard him leaving."

"Do you really think that Susan would admit that she heard him leaving even if he had?"

"What are you getting at? Do you think that Susan may be covering for Akard?"

"You don't think it's possible?"

Jack expelled a harsh breath and put the car in gear. "That's always a possibility and one that we'll need to rule out. Because if it does turn out that Akard's involved in this mess, that may make Susan an accomplice," he said just as his cell phone rang.

Jack recognized Ashley's voice immediately. "Hi, babe. What's up? Is everything okay?"

"Everything's fine. The reason I'm calling is because I thought you'd like to know that there's a press conference going on down at City Hall. The local news station is providing live coverage, and Steve Akard is there now."

"Press conference?"

"I'm not one hundred percent certain, but it looks like it's to clear up any rumors of corruption. Tom Oden is also there."

Jack glanced at the clock on the dashboard. "How long ago did it start?"

"About ten minutes ago. I called because I wasn't sure if you would want to attend."

"I do. Thanks for the heads up. And Ashley, don't call Susan and ask her to have lunch with you today. Not after what happened at Finnegan's house." He knew that there was a chance that the person who broke into Finnegan's house was beginning to get desperate. If it turned out to be Myers, Jack didn't want Ashley to have any interaction with her.

"Don't worry. I won't. I already decided against it."

"Good. I'll see you tonight," Jack said before disconnecting the call.

"What did Ashley say?" Ryan asked.

"There's a press conference going on now. Steve Akard and Tom Oden are there. Let's head over and see what's going on."

Twenty minutes later, Jack and Ryan were making their way into one of the press rooms at City Hall. The mayor was fielding questions from reporters while he gripped the sides of the podium, addressing the allegations of corruption within the local government.

Jack stood with his back to the wall, taking in the scene. Though there were several reporters that were vying for the man's attention, Jack had no problem in zeroing in on Akard. The man's distinct voice carried through the area, his voice practically vibrating through the room as he asked question after question about the allegations of corruption.

"He's very exuberant," Ryan observed.

"Yeah, he is."

"Do you think that's his normal style?"

"I'm not sure. I'll have to ask Ashley about it later."

"Didn't Ashley say that Tom Oden was supposed to be here?"

"She did." Jack scanned the room, trying to catch a glimpse of the man, but there were too many reporters mulling about, too many people jockeying for a better spot closer to the podium.

"I think I see him."

"Where?"

"Off to the right. Next to the photographer by the stage."

Jack glanced in the direction, and he caught a glimpse of Oden. "That's him," he said, observing the visible anger in his facial features. His eyes were narrowed, and even from a distance Jack could see the muscle ticking in the man's jaw.

"He looks angry," Ryan said.

"Yeah, he does." Jack caught sight of the man's fists clenching and unclenching by his side.

"The man's definitely bitter."

"The question is, who is he angry at?"

"It looks like the mayor."

"Does it? From his vantage point, he could be look-ing at Akard."

"Why would he have a problem with Akard?"

"Maybe he thinks that the man has access to Finnegan's notes. And if that's the case, we may be looking at the person who broke into Finnegan's early this morning."

Ryan continued to watch the man. "He's moving," he whispered as he saw Oden turn abruptly on his heel and head toward a side exit.

"I'm going to follow him," Jack said, quickly moving toward the exit that Oden was walking through.

Jack quickened his pace as he tried to keep up. Oden's stride was long and quick, and Jack couldn't help but wonder exactly what it was that he was rushing to.

As Jack made it to the door, he stopped short at the sound of angry voices. Two males were exchanging harsh words, and Jack paused. He recognized one of the voices as that of Oden, but he was having difficulty placing the other.

Easing the door open slightly, he glanced through the opening, being careful to stay hidden from view. He didn't want to announce his presence. Though he had no trouble identifying the underlying anger in the voices from both men, he couldn't make out enough of the words to determine why. Deciding to wait it out and see if they would say anything interesting, his plan abruptly changed when he saw the person reach out and roughly grab Oden's arm. Wanting to prevent a physical confrontation, Jack flung open the door and walked into the hallway.

Oden immediately glanced at Jack as he came into the hall, his eyes going wide at the sight of him. The arrested expression on his face must have caught the other man's attention because he immediately released Oden's arm and stopped speaking before he slowly turned. It was Drew Kaye.

Chapter Fifteen

"Detective Reeves," Tom Oden said as he quickly regained his wits.

Jack nodded. "Mr. Oden, Mr. Kaye." He tried to see if either one of them had a pierced ear. But he couldn't tell. Though neither man wore an earring, they were also too far away for him to notice any piercing of the skin.

"Detective," Kaye replied.

Oden looked at Jack curiously. "I didn't expect you to attend this press conference."

"I understand that if Frank Finnegan were alive, he would have been covering it," Jack said.

Kaye showed no outward response to the mention of Finnegan. Instead he prompted Jack to expand on his comment. "So?"

"So, I was wondering if perhaps the person who murdered Finnegan might show up here today."

"You think his murder is related to one of the stories he was covering?" Kaye asked.

Jack shrugged slightly. "It's a possibility." He watched Oden shift uncomfortably.

"I suppose it is."

"I didn't interrupt anything just now, did I?"

"Not at all. I was just leaving."

Oden cast a sharp look at Kaye, and for a moment Jack thought he would say something. But instead, he clenched his jaw shut and didn't say a word.

Jack addressed his next question to Kaye. "Do you mind if I ask you something before you go?"

Kaye cast a quick look at his watch before shrugging. "I suppose I have a few moments. What did you want to know?"

"I was wondering where you were around four o'clock this morning?"

Kaye stilled slightly, but it was the only outward sign that he was bothered by the question. "I was at home sleeping. Why are you asking?"

"There was a break-in at Frank Finnegan's house about that time."

"And you think I had something to do with that?"

"You tell me."

Kaye shook his head slightly. "Sorry. I have better things to do at that time. You'll have to look elsewhere for your answers."

Jack nodded and turned to Oden. The man had a slight sheen of sweat on his forehead, and Jack knew instinctively that he was uncomfortable. "And you, Mr. Oden? Where were you this morning?"

Oden took out his handkerchief and carefully blotted his forehead. "I was arguing with my wife."

Jack's eyes narrowed. "I thought you were separated."

"I'm trying to work on a reconciliation."

"But you just said you were arguing . . ."

"I said *I'm trying* to work on a reconciliation. I never said my wife was."

"Still, four o'clock in the morning is an odd time to be arguing."

Oden let out a gusty sigh. "I called her on the phone. I couldn't sleep and I knew she was an early riser. She has a habit of getting up at four o'clock to exercise. I wanted to catch her before she left for an early morning jog."

"I take it by your comment that you were arguing that she wasn't very receptive to the idea."

"Hardly. And I blame Finnegan for that. His lies poisoned my marriage. But as I told you the other day, I had absolutely nothing to do with Finnegan's death," Oden ground out harshly, his stress with the situation clearly evident.

"Your statement's duly noted." Jack couldn't help but notice the look of total loathing that Kaye shot at Oden.

Oden nodded. "Good. Then if you'll excuse me, I'll get back to the conference inside."

"Of course," Jack said, watching the man walk past him.

"He has a lot of anger," Kaye stated.

"It appears so."

"I guess I can't blame him."

"I imagine you have the same anger toward Finnegan."

"I never claimed not to."

"No, you haven't. Can I ask you one more thing?"

"Sure."

"What exactly are you doing here?"

"Here? You mean at the press conference?"

"Yeah. What's your interest here? I mean I know why Tom Oden's here. He probably has an interest in getting his job back. But you? What are you hoping to gain?"

"I'm not looking to gain anything. I am, however, hoping that my bids will be considered for future projects. It's why I came. To get a feel for the new council member."

"And what did you determine?"

"I think with time, things will calm down. That the council members will realize that Finnegan fabricated a lot of lies."

"You sound very sure of that."

"I am. The truth always wins out."

"I'm a firm believer in that also."

Kaye paused for a few moments. "I knew we had some things in common."

"I take it by the fact that you were getting ready to

leave that you already received the answer you were looking for from the press conference?"

"I did. The comment was made that no evidence had surfaced substantiating Finnegan's claim. It's only a matter of time before the damage that Finnegan did with his story will correct itself."

"If that's the case, why is Oden so angry with you?"

"He blames me for his troubles. I think he would be happy if I never submitted another bid to City Hall."

"Surely he can't hold you responsible for the article Finnegan wrote?"

"He does. No matter what evidence there is to the contrary, I'm afraid Oden will always believe that I somehow could have prevented Frank from writing that piece. He's angry that I even showed up here today. He thinks my presence here will just add fuel to Frank's allegations. Now if you'll excuse me, I need to be going."

"Of course. Thank you for your time."

Jack watched him leave before he went in search of Ryan. He found him standing in the same spot he had left him, watching the press conference.

"I was wondering where you disappeared to."

Jack expelled a short breath. "I found Oden talking to Drew Kaye out in the hallway."

Ryan's eyes widened. "Drew Kaye was here?"

"Yes, he was. And it looked like the two of them were having some harsh words. At least until I made my presence known."

"Interesting."

"Very."

"Were you able to get anything out of them?"

"Not much. Oden is still very bitter. And he was uncomfortable with my presence."

"Did you ask where he was this morning?" Ryan asked.

"He claimed arguing with his wife."

"That'll be easy enough to prove."

"I agree. And I think we should make contact with his wife just as soon as we leave here."

"I'm game," Ryan said, shifting slightly as a reporter jostled into him. "What else did you find out in the hallway?"

"Just that Kaye insists that all the allegations that Finnegan made were false. He's convinced that the truth will come out since no evidence has presented itself to suggest that the information Finnegan leaked was based on fact."

"I wonder if he believes that because he knows that any evidence to the contrary has already been taken care of."

"I'm wondering the same thing," Jack said.

"Just out of curiosity, what was his alibi for his whereabouts this morning?"

"He claims he was sleeping."

Ryan sighed. "A hard alibi to fight, especially for four o'clock in the morning."

"I agree. I don't think the district attorney will debate

that or ask for more proof. Not unless we had some serious evidence that would suggest otherwise." Jack paused before asking, "What did I miss here?"

"Not much. Oden came back in a short while ago and left almost immediately through a different door."

"Really."

"You sound surprised."

"I am a little.

"Why?" Ryan asked.

"The man said he wanted to come back and watch the rest of the press conference."

"Well, something obviously changed his mind."

"Yeah, but what?"

"Running into you perhaps?"

"Seems that way."

"So the question is, why?"

"And I think it's a question we need to work on getting the answer to today," Jack said, glancing at the activity still taking place. "What about Akard?"

"What about him?"

"How's he been behaving?"

"Like a reporter."

Jack smiled slightly. "He didn't seem to be acting strange?"

"No. He's asking all the right questions. To be honest, it doesn't look like he's trying to sensationalize anything. He's giving the impression that he just wants to present the facts."

"That's refreshing."

"Yeah. It would be interesting to know what his normal reporting tactics were," Ryan said.

"That's something that I can probably get an answer to."

"How?"

"How do you think?"

Ryan smiled slightly. "By asking Ashley?"

"She has access to a lot of information."

"That she does," Ryan said, glancing at his watch. "We still have a lot to do today. Are you about ready to go?"

Jack glanced around the room once more. "Yeah, I think we got all we can from here. Let's go see what else we can find."

Chapter Sixteen

Two hours later, Jack and Ryan were back at the police station. They had stopped and talked to Tom Oden's wife, Mary, and she confirmed that her husband had indeed called her at four o'clock that morning and that they had argued. But she said something else that Jack and Ryan found curious. She had mentioned that Oden had called her from his cell phone. A quick check had confirmed that. Which meant that Oden could have easily called from Frank Finnegan's house.

Ryan glanced at Jack. "We should go and check in with Ed."

"Yeah. Just give me a minute to get a cup of coffee," Jack said.

"Okay. While you're doing that, I'm going to run and get a soda."

Jack nodded and watched him go before moving to the coffee maker to pour himself a cup of the strong brew. Taking a sip, he made his way to his desk and phoned home.

"Hi, babe," Jack said the moment Ashley answered the phone.

"Jack. Hi. Did you make it to the press conference?"

"Yeah. That's why I'm calling actually."

"Oh?"

"I wanted to ask you how familiar you were with Steve Akard's interviewing style."

"What do you mean?"

"I know you said he was always in competition with Frank Finnegan, but I'm curious if he did it in a low-key way."

"I'm not sure I follow . . ."

"The guy was very professional. Very fair in his questioning, even though he was relentless in trying to get an honest response."

"He would be. That's the way he conducts himself."

"Always?"

"Any time I had the opportunity to watch. His reporting style was slightly different than Frank's."

Jack frowned. "What do you mean?"

"Frank was very hard-core. He's been known to exaggerate to get the best byline."

"What are you saying? That his facts aren't always right?"

"No. Don't get me wrong. He didn't lie or stretch the

truth. He just liked to put a different spin on it. He tried to sway public opinion. He was very good at it actually."

"Meaning he gave a lot of people cause to hate him."

"Basically, but you already knew that."

"Yeah."

"Are you going to be working late tonight?"

"A few more hours."

"Then I'll hold dinner for you."

"You don't have to. If you're hungry . . ."

"I can wait."

Jack smiled. "Okay. I'll see you soon."

"Soon," she said before saying good-bye and hanging up.

Jack took a sip of his coffee and swiveled slightly in his chair, thinking.

"What's up?" Ryan asked as he walked back into the room. Popping the top on his can of soda, he took a long sip.

"Ashley said that the way Akard conducted himself today was normal."

"Meaning he has honor as a reporter."

"It looks that way."

"A trait that it doesn't look like Frank Finnegan shared."

"It's something we have to keep in mind," Jack said just as Ed walked into the detectives' room.

"I'm glad you two are here. I have the preliminary reports from the break-in at Finnegan's on my desk. Let's go into my office and discuss them."

Jack reached for his coffee and followed Ed into his office with Ryan close on his heels.

"So, what did we come up with?" Jack asked as he took a seat.

Ed picked up a manila folder and passed it to Jack. "Look for yourself."

Jack shot him a brief look before opening the folder. He quickly read through the contents of the first page. "They found a blond hair in the ski cap."

"Yeah, but it doesn't match Susan's."

"What about Steve Akard?" Ryan asked.

Ed shrugged. "That we're not sure of. We didn't have anything to compare it to that we could identify as his."

"Drew Kaye has blond hair," Jack said.

"So did Tom's wife, Mary," Ryan reminded him.

Jack grunted. "So without a definite suspect, we still don't have much to go on."

"Unfortunately, I have to agree with that," Ed said.

"What about the earring?" Jack asked as he flipped through the remainder of the report, looking for a notation.

"It's still being tested," Ed replied. "It'll be a while before we get the results back. Did you happen to notice if anyone had a pierced ear in your travels today?"

"Susan did. We even thought it belonged to her for a brief while today," Jack revealed.

"Oh?"

"She was wearing a diamond stud earring when we got to her apartment this morning."

"Just one?"

"Just one. I thought for sure we had her until she found the other one."

"Meaning, we pretty much have to clear her."

"Unless she realized it was missing and had a spare . . ."

Ed shook his head. "The diamond we found was real and high quality. The chances of her having two identical sets are slim."

Jack finished looking through the file and handed it to Ryan. "Did anything else come in today?"

"No, just that. We should be getting a few more pieces of information tomorrow. The evidence collected didn't point to anything obvious. It'll take a while to sort through it."

Jack grunted. "We came up with some interesting facts today."

"Such as?"

"Such as the fact that a press conference was held down at City Hall discussing the corruption that Frank Finnegan had reported on."

"Who was there?"

"Steve Akard, Tom Oden, and Drew Kaye."

Ed let out a soft whistle. "Anything come from it?"

"Oden and Kaye have a bit of a rocky relationship."

"Any idea why?"

"Not sure. According to Drew, Tom blames him entirely for his troubles. And I have to say if Oden was truly throwing business Kaye's way, he didn't give any indication of it. There was absolutely no camaraderie between the two of them."

Ed was silent. "That could just be the result of everything going sour."

"Possibly."

"Anything else?"

Ryan nodded. "While Jack was outside with Oden and Kaye, I had the opportunity to watch Steve Akard in action."

"And?"

"And the man handled himself very professionally. He didn't look like he was trying to prove anything."

"He's been in the business a long time."

"True. But still . . ."

"You don't see anything there."

"Very little. I think we still need to keep an eye on him, but I'm not getting a strong feeling that he was involved in Finnegan's murder."

"So, we'll keep searching."

"That's about all we can do," Jack said.

Ed nodded. "Tomorrow's another day. With a little luck, we'll get some more forensics reports in, and maybe we'll get a break that will help us determine which direction we should go."

"Anything else we need to cover tonight?"

Ed shook his head and sorted through a few more reports. "No. Nothing that's going to help."

"Then if it's okay with you, Ryan and I will call it a day."

"Sure. You've both been putting in a lot of hours lately."

"It's all part of the job," Jack said.

"The hard part."

"Yeah. But at the end of the day, you feel good that you're doing something to make things right. To remove the people from the street that have no business in the population."

"That's a cynical thought."

"But a true one."

"I can't argue," Ed said. "So, I'll see you tomorrow morning, bright and early."

"Tomorrow," Ryan agreed.

"I'll meet you both down here at eight," Jack said as he got to his feet.

Chapter Seventeen

Dusk was beginning to fall as Jack pulled into the driveway. The moment he parked the car, the front door opened and Ashley came out with John, who was waving. A smile came over Jack's face as he waved back. Turning off the engine, he reached for his suit jacket from the passenger seat and exited the car.

"Hey," he greeted as John came running over to him. Bending down, he scooped the toddler into his arms and hugged him. "I missed you, pal."

"I missed you," John said, hugging him tightly.

Jack rubbed John's back as he walked over to Ashley. He bent down to kiss her. "Hi."

"Hi, back."

"How was your day?"

"Pretty good. And yours?"

"Can't complain," he said as he began walking toward the front door with her. "You mentioned something about holding dinner earlier?"

"I did."

"What did you have in mind?"

"I thought we would grill if it's okay."

"Sounds good to me. I didn't have time for lunch today, so I'm starving."

Ashley shot him a look. "I'm sure you could have taken a few minutes to eat."

"Actually, no."

"It was that hectic today?"

"It was. Do I have time for a quick shower?"

She smiled. "Of course you do. I think I can keep John occupied for ten minutes."

Jack laughed down at his son who was holding onto him for dear life. "If you're sure . . ."

Ashley reached for John, gently prying him from Jack's embrace. "I think I can manage."

"I won't be long," Jack promised as John continued to reach for him.

"We'll be in the kitchen."

Fifteen minutes later, Jack walked into the kitchen dressed in gym shorts and a T-shirt. John was coloring at the table and Ashley was by the sink scrubbing potatoes. He smiled at the picture they made.

"Here's my family," he said, tousling his son's hair before walking over to Ashley and hugging her. He breathed in the sweet smell of her perfume. "I missed you today."

"I missed you too."

Jack looked at the counter. He saw the steaks that were marinating, the salad that she had prepared, and the pitcher of ice tea. "You've been busy."

"I had to do something while we were waiting for you," she teased.

"What can I do to help?"

Ashley glanced lovingly at their son. "I know John would love for you to color with him."

Jack smiled and glanced over at his son who was smiling broadly at him. "Is that true?"

John nodded and, jumping down from the chair, he ran to Jack and grabbed his hand. "Yeah."

Jack laughed. "Then I guess that's what I'll do."

Ashley smiled as she watched the two men in her life get settled. "So tell me, did you come up with anything this afternoon?"

"Not much."

"I talked to one of my contacts down at the newspaper this afternoon."

Jack looked up. "Oh?"

"She mentioned that Steve Akard really wasn't interested in taking over the story about the corruption down at City Hall."

"He wasn't?"

"No. She said that he went out of his way to convince the editor that someone else should cover the story."

"That's interesting," Jack murmured.

Ashley nodded slightly and gave the potatoes one final rinse before she popped them in the microwave and set the timer. "I thought so too."

"She didn't happen to say why by any chance, did she?"

Ashley turned and leaned against the counter. "She's not a hundred percent sure, but she thinks it has something to do with Susan Myers."

"In what way?"

"Apparently Susan is so upset over Frank's murder, that Steve feels bad capitalizing on it."

"So the guy has genuine feelings for her."

"It appears so."

"Did your friend say anything else?"

"Just that Susan's really traumatized. She doesn't want to go back to work. She feels really bad that her phone cord was used to strangle Frank."

"She said that?"

"Yeah. According to my friend, Susan is taking an unspecified leave of absence. She said she wouldn't be surprised if she gave her notice."

"That seems a little drastic," Jack said.

"I agree. But everybody deals with stress in different ways. I don't know why, but I honestly don't believe that Susan had anything to do with Frank Finnegan's murder."

Jack was quiet for a moment. "I don't either. But I don't have any evidence that would preclude her from being a suspect."

"I think I might."

Jack gave her a sharp look. "What?"

"I don't have anything based on fact, just hearsay."

"What is it, Ashley?"

"The friend I was talking to today mentioned that one of the other people in the building had been talking."

"About?"

"About his supposed relationship with Susan Myers. Apparently, Susan had begun seeing another man down at the newspaper."

"How does that preclude her from being a suspect?"

"Apparently the two of them were talking to one another at the time Frank was murdered."

"Nobody said anything to that effect," Jack said.

"They wouldn't."

"Why not?"

"Susan was afraid that Steve would find out."

"Why?"

"He's still in love with her."

Jack sat back in his chair. "If that's the case, why is this guy talking now?"

"He's not exactly talking . . ."

Jack shook his head slightly in confusion. "Then I don't understand where this is all coming from."

"Jack, you know as well as I do that rumors and gossip run rampant in workplaces."

"So?"

"Apparently this guy overheard a couple of people talking about Susan being a suspect. They found out about the search that was done at her house."

"I'm sorry about that," Jack said, knowing it was beyond his control.

"Anyway, he jumped to Susan's defense. He said that there was no way she could be responsible for Frank Finnegan's murder because she was on the phone with him."

"Is the guy trustworthy?"

"I would say so."

"Who is he?"

"Brent Jones. The director of security."

"Jones," Jack repeated, flashing back to the night when Finnegan was murdered. He recalled meeting the man. He seemed very willing to help with the investigation, but now Jack had to question why. Was he truly interested in helping the police, or was he more concerned that no suspicion be focused on him? Because the fact of the matter was that if Jones was seeing Myers, he may have had his own motive for wanting to see Finnegan dead.

"Jack?"

Jack's attention was diverted to the present. "Yeah?"

"Are you okay?"

"I am, but I think I'll have to go out after dinner."

"To talk to Brent?"

"Yeah. There's a lot of blanks that need to be filled in. I'm sorry to have to cut out on you."

"It's okay. I understand."

Jack looked down at his son and ran a hand gently over his hair. "I hope you understand too."

"Don't worry about, John. He'll be fine."

Jack looked at Ashley. "When this is all over, I'll make it up to you. To both of you."

"What did you have in mind?"

"A long weekend at Montauk?"

"Sounds heavenly."

"Then that's what we'll do. John loves the sand and water. He should have a ball."

"He'll be happy just being with you."

"I hope so."

"He will," she said just as the microwave buzzer sounded. "We should get ready to go outside."

Jack stood and picked up John. "I'll get the steaks."

Chapter Eighteen

A few hours later, Jack had met up with Ryan and they were on their way to talk to Brent Jones.

Ryan shifted into a more comfortable position in the passenger seat of Jack's car. "I have to tell you, I was surprised to learn that Jones is involved with Susan Myers."

"You can't be more surprised than I was when Ashley mentioned it."

"The man never gave a clue."

Jack shot Ryan a quick look. "Neither did Susan."

"Yeah. But from her, I kind of understand it."

"What do you mean?"

"I mean Steve Akard has been hanging around her. It makes sense that she wouldn't bring up the subject of another man."

157

"Maybe," Jack conceded.

"Don't get me wrong. I'm not excusing the fact that she kept this a secret, but I can't say I blame her."

"If it turns out that Jones was responsible for Finnegan's murder, I'll do more than blame her. I'll make sure she's charged as an accomplice."

Ryan grunted. "I think that's his place up ahead."

Jack looked at the house on the right that they were about to pull up to when he noticed a car by the curb. "It looks like he may have company."

Ryan's eyes narrowed as he caught sight of the car. "Either that or someone's watching the place."

"What makes you say that?"

"The driver looks like he's staring at the house."

"Interesting," Jack murmured, reaching for his cell. He quickly dialed the precinct to run a check on the license plate. After a couple of minutes, he disconnected the call and turned to Ryan. "You're not going to believe who the car belongs to."

"Who?"

"Drew Kaye."

Ryan was quiet for a moment. "Maybe they're friends."

"They're something, but the question is, what?"

"I don't think we're going to find out tonight."

"What makes you say that?"

"He's leaving," Ryan said, watching as the sedan sprang to life and pulled away.

"We'll have to see if Brent Jones will be as reticent

about his association with Drew Kaye as he was with Susan Myers."

"And if he is?"

"Then we'll have to get the answers from Kaye," Jack said as he parked the car, undid his seatbelt, and opened the door.

The outside porch light came on when they were within fifteen feet of the door, and Jack guessed that it was triggered by a sensor. There also was a strong bark coming from inside the home to alert the occupant of their presence.

"Quiet, Max," an authoritive voice boomed before the front door was pulled open to reveal Jones.

Jones's eyes narrowed slightly. "Detective Reeves. Detective Parks."

"Mr. Jones, we were wondering if we could have a moment of your time," Jack said.

Jones glanced at his watch. "It's kind of late."

"We realize that, but we won't stay long. And since you just recently had company . . ."

"Company?"

"Yes. There was a car by your curb. We just assumed the person had been visiting you."

Jones's eyes narrowed to mere slits as he stepped outside and began glancing around at the dark street. "Nobody was here."

Jack's curiosity about Kaye was further piqued. "Maybe the person was visiting someone else."

"Maybe," Jones said before turning his attention back

to Jack and Ryan. "As long as you're here, why don't you come in."

"Thank you. As I said, we'll try not to take up too much of your time."

"I'm not ready for sleep yet," Jones assured them as he held the German shepherd's collar while they entered the house.

Jack immediately let the dog smell his hand before he petted him. "You have a beautiful dog."

"Thanks. I had him since he was a pup. Please, take a seat," Jones said, motioning to the sofa. "I'm sorry if I seemed a little short earlier. You caught me off guard stopping by like this."

"It's understandable."

"So tell me, what can I do for you?"

Jack glanced at Ryan. "We understand that you made a comment publicly that you were speaking to Susan Myers at the time of Finnegan's murder."

Jones flushed. "That's correct."

"Can I ask how you can be so certain that you were talking to her during the exact time of Finnegan's death?"

"I'm not."

"Then perhaps you can explain your comment."

Jones ran an agitated hand through his hair. "Susan and I are friends. She was working a little later than normal that evening to make up some hours that she had missed earlier in the week due to taking some time off because her mother was hospitalized. She called me on my cell phone after I left for the day to see if I wanted to have lunch tomorrow. When I had another call come in, I put her on hold and took it. It was one of my security guards. The one who found the body."

"Why didn't you mention this the other night?"

"I didn't think it was important. At least not until I realized she was considered a suspect in Finnegan's murder."

"Are you dating Susan Myers?" Jack asked bluntly, needing to know just how far the man would go to protect her.

"Susan and I are friends."

"That's not what I asked."

Jones frowned. "You think she and I are romantically involved?"

"Are you?"

"No!"

"Were you ever?"

"I admit I considered asking her out, but I never acted on it."

"Why?"

"Workplace romances never work."

"You sound like you speak from experience," Ryan said.

"I do. I met my first wife on the job."

"Your first wife? I take it you're divorced?"

"You take it right. And it was a bitter end. It's difficult enough when you have problems. But when they start playing out in front of your colleagues . . ."

"It's rough. We understand," Ryan assured him.

Jones was quiet for a moment. "I can't say I'm really surprised that the rumors are flying down at the paper regarding a relationship between Susan and myself."

"Why's that?" Jack asked.

"Because we're friends. Close friends. But nothing more, and nothing less. It's the main reason I couldn't stand by and watch her take the heat for Frank Finnegan's murder. I would stake my life that she would never hurt the man. She knew about his faults and accepted them. She didn't have it in her to kill him."

"You sound very sure of that."

"I'm very sure of Susan. She handles herself with grace regardless of what curveballs life throws at her."

"You respect her," Jack said.

"I do."

"We appreciate your honesty."

"I told you I would help in any way I can with this investigation, and I meant it."

"Can I ask you something?"

"Sure."

"When was the last time you saw Drew Kaye?"

Jones frowned. "Drew? I saw him this afternoon down at the newspaper. Why do you ask?"

Jack shrugged. "Just curious. Do you mind if I ask what he was doing down at the newspaper?"

"I'm not sure exactly, but from my understanding he was trying to get Finnegan's editor to write a retraction on the article that accused him and Tom Oden of corruption."

"Did he have any luck?"

"The files that Frank had on the case are missing. They seemed to have vanished. Unless the paper can find them, I don't think they'll have any choice but to print the retraction."

"Do you think the files were kept in his desk at the paper?"

"Like I said, if they were, we can't find them. One of my men broke the lock on his desk to gain access. There was nothing there. As a matter of fact, we were searching the desk when Drew was there."

Jack couldn't help but wonder if that was the reason Kaye had been outside Jones's home. If Kaye was at *The Chronicle* when Finnegan's desk was being searched, he would have been concerned that the files or duplicate files would have been found, which would ruin any chance for a retraction. And if that was the case, he might have been thinking of an excuse to approach Jones to find out for sure.

"Do you think it's possible that Frank kept the files at his house?" Jack asked, thinking about the break-in at the man's home.

"It would be my guess. Though I have to say, Frank had a reputation for being a stickler for keeping his sources sacred. I'm sure if he had files, he also had them backed up somewhere."

"On a personal computer?" Jack asked, knowing that Finnegan's was taken into evidence. Though they hadn't located any files yet, they had their experts working on the hard drive to see if they were there and if they could be retrieved.

"I think I mentioned during our first meeting that Frank and I socialized together. Even though I didn't work directly with him, I knew him well enough to know that he was very hi-tech and just a bit paranoid. I'm quite sure he had them on some sort of storage device hidden in a safe location."

"What do you mean by paranoid?"

Jones shrugged. "He was always worried that someone was going to get a jump on one of his stories."

"But I don't understand. Weren't they assigned to specific individuals?"

"They were. But reporting is a very competitive game. There's no room for carelessness. Your facts and your sources must be protected at all costs. But I'm sure you already know that from living with Ashley."

"You're right, I do."

"I'm quite sure Frank's files are safe and sound somewhere. I don't think he was into fabricating stories."

"Well, we thank you for your time. We'll be in touch in case anything else comes up. We'll see ourselves out."

The moment Jack and Ryan were back in the car, Ryan spoke. "So what do you think?"

"I think we'd better get a search warrant for Drew Kaye's house as soon as possible."

"I agree."

"I'll call Ed and get the ball rolling. I want access to his place by morning."

"It'll be hard to get a judge at this hour," Ryan warned.

"Ed has a lot of people that owe him favors. He'll just have to put on some heat."

Chapter Nineteen

It was just before six in the morning when Jack, Ryan, and a search team arrived at Drew Kaye's house. Ed had managed to get a judge to sign off on the search warrant prior to the morning rush hour in an effort to catch Kaye before he left for work. Ed had also obtained a warrant for Kaye's office, and another team had already been dispersed to the location.

"A car's here," Ryan said, spotting a four-door brown sedan in the driveway.

Jack glanced at the license plate. "It's the same one that was parked outside Brent Jones's house." He parked. "I guess it's time to see what kind of reception we're going to receive."

"Let's go."

Jack rang the doorbell and it took only a minute for Kaye to answer the summons.

"Detective Reeves, Detective Parks. What can I do for you?" Kaye's surprise at finding them on his doorstep was evident in his voice.

Jack pulled out the warrant. "Mr. Kaye, we have a warrant to search your home."

"My home?" His body shifted slightly, almost as if he was trying to block them from entering.

Jack slowly slid a foot across the threshold. He could tell that their presence and his words had a profound effect on the man, and he didn't want to give Kaye any opportunity to try and close the door on them. Though the man wouldn't be successful in keeping them out, especially since they had a warrant, he had no desire to make this any more difficult than this was. "Yes. And I should warn you that there's another team searching your office."

Kaye frowned. "Why?"

"You're under suspicion for the murder of Frank Finnegan."

Kaye leaned weakly against the doorjamb. "What?"

"We believe you had a motive to want Frank Finnegan dead."

"You're crazy," Kaye whispered.

"If you're innocent, you have nothing to worry about. If you're not . . ."

"I'm calling my lawyer," Kaye stated harshly.

Jack nodded. "That's your prerogative, however, it won't prevent either search from taking place," he said before giving the signal for the search team to begin.

Kaye had no choice but to take a step back as his house was taken over by the crime scene investigators. With a look of near panic on his face, he quickly walked over to the phone and dialed his attorney.

Jack barely spared him a glance as the search begun, but the moment Kaye hung up the phone, he had Jack's full attention.

"My attorney will be here momentarily."

"As you wish. Tell me, Mr. Kaye, why exactly were you parked in front of Brent Jones's home last night?"

"I was visiting the man."

"That's funny. He didn't mention that."

"Maybe it's because he has something to hide."

"Or maybe you do."

Kaye's eyes narrowed. "Exactly what are you implying?"

"We understand you paid a visit to Frank Finnegan's editor yesterday looking for a retraction."

"So?"

"So we also understand that you were asking for that due to the fact that there was no evidence to support the article that Finnegan wrote. The one that ruined your career."

"There isn't. I'm within my rights to ask for the retraction."

"That's true. You are within your rights. But the question is, is there no evidence because you broke into Finnegan's house and stole it?"

Kaye paled slightly at the accusation, but it was the only indication he gave that he was disconcerted. "I don't know what you're talking about."

"Don't you?"

"No."

Jack stared at him for a moment before gesturing toward the chairs in the living room. "Can we sit?"

"I really don't have anything to say without my attorney present."

"Are you sure about that? If you answer everything honestly, if you truly have nothing to hide, we can have the questioning completed without your attorney, and possibly put an end to this before it goes any further."

"Is that true? Or is that just some way to try and trap me into confessing to something that I didn't do?"

"If you didn't do it, there's no way to trap you."

"And if I don't talk?"

"If you don't talk, then we continue this conversation down at the precinct. And you would be wise to have your attorney present."

Kaye's eyes narrowed. "That sounds like a threat, Detective."

"It's just the truth."

"I had nothing to do with the break-in at Frank Finnegan's house."

"Then you won't mind telling us why you were outside of Brent Jones's house last night."

"I already told you."

"And I already said that Mr. Jones disputes that claim. And quite frankly, I'm inclined to believe him."

"Why would you do that? Aren't you supposed to keep an open mind?" Kaye asked, beginning to pace impatiently.

"I always keep an open mind."

"Except in this case. Why are you so sure that I had something to do with Finnegan's murder?"

"You had motive and opportunity."

"So did a lot of people."

"That's true, but you were a little sloppy. Do you even realize that you lost your ski cap the night that you were at Finnegan's place? And that several strands of hair were attached to the cap? Hair that we'll now be able to match to yours?" he asked, taking a calculated risk and releasing the information in an effort to get the man to confess.

When Kaye didn't immediately answer, Jack took a moment to study him. The man's stone face gave away nothing.

"No comment?" Jack asked.

"There's nothing to say."

Jack continued to stare at him for a moment before his attention was diverted by Ryan waving him over. With a brief nod to Ryan, he looked back at Kaye. "I'm going to leave you alone for a few moments to think about how you want this to play out," he said, getting up and leaving the room.

"What did you find?" Jack asked the moment he was by Ryan's side.

Ryan held up a small plastic evidence bag. "This."

Jack frowned as he studied the small diamond stud. It looked like a match to the one picked up at Finnegan's house. "Where's the other one?"

"That's it. Its twin's not here."

"Maybe that's because it's being held in evidence."

"That was my thought."

"Did we come up with anything else that we can tie to Finnegan's house?"

"If you're referring to files, no."

Jack grunted. "Even if we can tie this earring and Drew Kaye to the break-in at Finnegan's, it's a long stretch to tie him to Finnegan's murder."

"We have nothing else to go on," Ryan said just as Jack's cell phone rang.

Jack listened briefly. After a couple of minutes of conversation, he disconnected the call.

"Who was it?"

"The CSI team at Drew Kaye's office."

"And?"

"And they found files that look like they belong to Finnegan. They also found his briefcase."

"In Kaye's office?"

"Yeah. They were locked in a credenza."

Ryan whistled softly. "We can proceed with that."

"It's all circumstantial. We need more to lock this case."

"You want to get a confession."

"Yeah, I do. And I think the best place to get that would be on our turf," Jack replied.

"Down at the precinct?"

"We'll have an advantage."

Ryan nodded and motioned to the front door. "It looks like Kaye's attorney just arrived."

Jack turned and watched as a harried-looking man quickly gained access to the house and, after a glance around at the proceedings, went in search of his client. "He looks a little flustered."

"I was just thinking the same thing."

"I'll go and break the news that this conversation will be continuing down at the police station."

"I'll stay here and make sure that there's nothing else that we can use to tie the man to Finnegan."

"All right," Jack said, barely sparing Ryan a glance as he made his way to where Kaye and his attorney stood speaking in low, hushed tones.

"Mr. Kaye," Jack called out as he approached the two men.

"Detective Reeves, this is my attorney, Sam Woods."

Jack turned to Woods. "Mr. Woods, I'm glad you're here."

"Good. Because your harassment of my client is about to stop. I'm asking you to leave."

"I will, but you'll both be accompanying me down to the station," Jack told him. "Mr. Kaye, you're under arrest for the murder of Frank Finnegan."

Chapter Twenty

It was an hour later before everybody was seated in one of the interrogation rooms at the precinct. Drew Kaye sat by his attorney, but his nerves were showing. The man repeatedly ran his hand through his hair, and weary lines of fatigue were noticeable around his eyes and mouth. Though it was barely nine, Kaye looked as if he had been up all night.

Sam Woods, Kaye's attorney, looked at Jack and Ryan. "Detectives, I have yet to see any evidence that would suggest my client was responsible for the murder of Frank Finnegan."

Jack shot him a brief glance before focusing on Kaye. "We found an earring at Finnegan's house that's a match to one found at Mr. Kaye's. We also found files belonging to Finnegan at your client's office. Tell me, Mr. Kaye,

173

can you explain how you came to be in possession of those items?"

Kaye shook his head slightly. "I don't know what you're talking about."

"Don't you?" Jack asked, reaching for a large bag and slowly removing the evidence which was protected by clear plastic bags. "Does anything here look familiar to you?" he asked, spreading out the ski mask, both earrings, Finnegan's briefcase, and a portable USB device.

Kaye paled at the sight of the items, and he closed his eyes for a moment as he tried to get his bearings. After a minute of silence, he spoke. "One of the earrings is mine, but I never wear it. The people I deal with can be very conservative when it comes to men wearing earrings."

"What about the twin?" Jack asked, ignoring his comment about not wearing the earring. He suspected it was only said to draw attention away from the find. The man had to have realized that he lost the earring at Finnegan's house.

"It was only a single earring. It was given to me by a girlfriend."

Jack had to give the man credit for his quick thinking. "You won't mind supplying her name then, so my partner can go check it out? It won't take long. We can wait here."

Kaye gave a slight shrug. "I'm afraid she left town years ago. I haven't seen her since, and I have no forwarding information."

"How convenient," Jack murmured, maintaining eye contact with the man.

"Sorry I can't help."

"I wouldn't go that far. We have plenty more to discuss. Tell me, how did Finnegan's briefcase come to be at your office?"

"What makes you think it's Frank's?"

"Are you saying it's yours?"

When Kaye didn't respond, Jack pressed. "Perhaps you can explain what Frank's monogram is doing on the outside lock," he said, turning the briefcase around so that the man could get a good look at the initials.

"No?" Jack asked when Kaye remained quiet. "Maybe you can explain why Frank's personal papers are inside. Or how you came upon the USB device that has information on the article Frank wrote about you and corruption, and the papers that support his claim."

Kaye's jaw was beginning to clench. "I don't know what you're talking about."

"You keep telling yourself that and you might just believe it."

"What exactly do you want from me, Detective?"

"How about a confession that you killed Frank Finnegan in cold blood," Jack stated, watching as he paled at the words.

Kaye's eyes narrowed and he pushed his chair back from the table, the legs scraping harshly against the floor.

"You seem a little upset, Mr. Kaye," Jack observed.

"I'm being accused of murder. That tends to upset me."

"I'm not accusing you," Jack assured him.

Kaye laughed without humor. "You're not?"

"No. I know you killed Frank Finnegan. I just want you to admit it."

"Now see here—" Woods began.

Kaye held up a hand to stop him. "No, it's okay, Sam. Detective Reeves is so sure that I'm the one who killed Frank, let him prove it."

"Are you challenging me?" Jack asked, seeing the desperation on his features that he couldn't hide.

"If you're so sure . . ."

Jack stared at him for a moment longer before nodding. "All right. Let's start with the way you visited Finnegan's editor in an effort to get the retraction. You claimed they had to print it since there was no evidence to support it. But yet all we have to do is look down at this table to know otherwise. Tell me, why did you hold onto the evidence that you tried so hard to cover up? Was it your ego? Did you want a reminder of just how clever you were? Is that why you didn't destroy it?"

Kaye jumped up from the chair, knocking it over. Flushing slightly, he quickly righted it. "I don't know what you're talking about."

Jack didn't break eye contact. "We both know that's a lie. Face it, Mr. Kaye. You were caught red-handed with evidence that only Finnegan's murderer would have. Tell me why you did it. Was it the rage you felt to-

ward Finnegan that caused you to snap? Or was it something else? Did you feel euphoric once you took the
man's life?"

"I'm not a cold-blooded killer," Kaye insisted, his
breathing harsh and labored.

"The evidence suggests otherwise."

Kaye leaned into the chair, his knuckles turning
white as he gripped the back. "Let me say this clearly. I
did not kill Frank Finnegan."

"Then explain to me how you came to be in possession of his briefcase."

"I found it. By the dumpster in back of the newspaper."

"That's a lie," Jack charged. "The body was barely
cold by the time the police arrived on the scene. We
searched the entire area. You could only have come by the
briefcase if you were at the newspaper when Finnegan
was murdered. Stop playing games and talk to me. This
will all be a lot easier if you just cooperate."

Just then his cell phone rang. Jack quickly answered.
After a minute, he disconnected. Leaning back in his
chair, he studied Kaye. He noticed the beads of perspira-
tion on the man's brow, the ticking muscle in his tightly
clenched jaw. "That was the lab. The hair on the ski mask
is a match to yours. Are you still going to try to convince
me that you had nothing to do with Finnegan's murder?
That you didn't break into his house?"

He didn't immediately respond. Jack prompted, "Mr.
Kaye?"

Kaye ran a shaky hand through his hair. A full minute

passed before he admitted, "I was at his house. Frank had something of mine that I wanted to retrieve."

Jack's eyes narrowed slightly. "What?"

"He had taken a file from my office."

"What did the file contain?"

"Personal papers."

"What kind of papers?" Jack pressed, seeing the man tense as he looked at his attorney. Though no words were spoken, Jack sensed that Kaye was seeking some sort of guidance.

Kaye maintained eye contact with his attorney for a little longer before he turned back to Jack. "Frank stole a folder from my office that contained the bid I submitted to City Hall."

Jack sensed that the information in the folder was the key to this whole mess. "Did the file contain the proof that you had bribed Tom Oden? Was the information we found in Frank's briefcase the papers that he had taken from your office?"

"I never bribed Tom!"

There was something about the way he made the statement that had Jack looking at him curiously. "But you tried to," he guessed.

"No."

"Yes. And that's where all this is stemming from," Jack said, realizing he had hit upon the truth by the way Kaye paled. Though the man was doing his best to keep his composure, his body language was giving him away.

"I did not try to bribe Oden," Kaye ground out between clenched teeth.

"You're lying. You did try, but Oden wasn't interested. Isn't that right? And that's really the true reason you had to lowball your bid. To save face. To make sure that it never got out that you had tried to buy a city official. You knew that if you bid low enough, Oden would have no choice but to accept your numbers. The way the city's crunching numbers, you knew they couldn't afford to turn it down. And once Oden accepted the bid, he would have to keep his mouth shut about what you had tried to do."

"No!"

"Yes! And when Frank Finnegan found out about it, he exploited it," Jack concluded, as the pieces of the puzzle began to fall into place. "That's the true reason Oden's so angry with you. Because even though he didn't assign the bid to you because of any bribe, Frank's story gave everybody the impression that he did. You were careless, and your carelessness cost him his job and his marriage."

Kaye was shaking his head, too enraged to even speak, and Jack decided to capitalize on it. He knew that Kaye was so off kilter at the moment that it wouldn't take much to push him to the edge. "And then there's Frank Finnegan. The man responsible for all the grief in your life. The man who took your own information and turned it against you. You're losing clients because of that article, aren't you? Finnegan effectively ruined your business."

Kaye's breathing was becoming erratic. "I did not kill Frank Finnegan!" he spit out from behind clenched teeth.

"Yes, you did."

"No!"

"Detective—" Woods said before being cut off by Jack.

"You were at the newspaper the day Finnegan was killed. And you were angry that day. The surveillance tape that recorded your meeting with Frank is proof of that. Tell me, Mr. Kaye, did you go to *The Chronicle* with the intention of killing Finnegan? Or was that a decision you made after you spoke with him?"

Kaye kept shaking his head. "You don't know what you're talking about."

"Oh, but I do. A picture is worth a thousand words, and the tape of you and Frank arguing is priceless. The jury will have no doubt about the nature of your meeting with him. What happened? What caused you to snap? How did you somehow manage to stick around without being found out? Where did you hide? The stairway corridor? A stall in the men's room? A supply closet? Where exactly did you hide?"

When Kaye didn't respond, Jack knew he would have to push harder. "You waited around until every-body left, knowing that you would have the perfect opportunity to kill Finnegan. You knew he would be alone and that his guard would be down."

"No! You don't understand."

"Yes, I do. Your story's no different than anyone else's. Except yours points to premeditation. You knew the man had enemies. You thought you would never get caught. That there were too many other people that the finger of guilt would point to. So you waited until everybody had left the floor before you made your move. You took the phone cord from Susan Myers's phone, knowing that you were going to strangle Finnegan with it."

"I did not murder Frank!"

"You did! I know it, and you know it. And you did it in cold blood. Like a coward, you waited until the man was alone."

Jack's last statement made Kaye slam his fist on the table. "I wasn't the coward, Finnegan was. He didn't have the guts to tell the truth, so he created a story that ruined several lives. And he never had the nerve to face me after that."

"Except that he didn't create the story, you did. And even though you never proceeded with the bribe, you were still being blamed as if you did. And that bothered you."

"It would bother anyone."

"But it bothered you so much that you wanted revenge. You wanted the man to pay for what he did. To suffer. So you decided to take his life."

"He took mine!"

"So that justified your actions?" Jack pressed, knowing Kaye was close to breaking.

"Drew, don't say anything more," Woods warned.

Kaye barely spared him a glance. His face was mottled with rage as he answered Jack's attack. "Frank Finnegan was scum."

"He didn't deserve to die," Jack countered.

"He didn't care who he hurt."

"So that gave you justification to hurt him?"

"I tried to reason with him that day. I practically begged him to retract the story. He just laughed in my face. The man had no conscience."

"And that enraged you," Jack said, beginning to get a clear picture of how everything played out. "You wanted revenge."

"I wanted to wipe that smug expression off of his face."

"So you did."

Kaye didn't even appear to hear Jack. He was lost in his own world. "Even when he saw me by the elevator, he had that smug expression. Like he was better than me. Like nothing could touch him."

"And you wanted to prove him wrong."

"I wanted him to pay," Kaye countered roughly, his breathing harsh and shallow. "I needed him to pay. He took everything from me. I spent my life building up my business, and he thought nothing of destroying it! To him, it was a game. A byline to sell papers. Finnegan couldn't care less about truth and justice. You don't think he bought his share of stories? That he wasn't corrupt? Do I need to remind you that he stole that file from my office? He always thought that he was better than everybody else. That he was beyond the law. That he had some given right to pass judgment on people."

"So you decided to pass your own judgment," Jack said, feeling the rage emanating from Kaye.

"I decided to show Frank that he wasn't invincible," Kaye sneered bitterly. "That there were consequences for his actions. That he didn't have the right to destroy people's lives on a whim."

"So you killed him."

Woods stood. "Enough!" He turned to Kaye. "If you say one more word, I'm resigning as your attorney," he stated, looking as if he was prepared to forcibly keep him quiet.

Kaye looked at Woods, and the enormity of what just occurred, of his words, began to sink in. He closed his eyes in despair.

Jack watched him, wondering if he would say anything more. When it became apparent that he wasn't going to, he cast a glance at Ryan. "Do you want to take Mr. Kaye down to be processed?"

"Yeah," Ryan said, standing and waiting for Kaye and his attorney to do the same.

"I'll meet you down there in a few minutes. I'm going to go and fill Ed in."

Jack found Ed in his office.

Ed leaned back in his chair. "Well? How did it go with Drew Kaye?"

"We have him."

Ed sighed with relief. "He confessed?"

"There's no doubt that he's the one who murdered Finnegan. The man had a lot of anger toward Finnegan. My guess is he just exploded."

Ed nodded. "I'll call the district attorney and let him know."

"While you're doing that, I'll go and check in on Ryan and then get started on typing up the report to close the case." He turned to leave.

"Jack?"

He glanced over his shoulder. "Yeah?"

"You and Ryan did good," Ed told him gruffly.

"Thanks. I'll see you when I'm done with the report."

Jack found Ryan down in booking. "Everything okay?"

Ryan ran a weary hand around his neck. "Yeah. Kaye's being fingerprinted as we speak."

"Did he say anything else?"

"He's not talking. His attorney's making sure of that."

"No surprise there," Jack murmured, watching as several officers stood guard by Kaye. "It looks like they have everything under control. Why don't we go back upstairs and get started on the paperwork so that we can put this case to bed."

"Sounds good."

Chapter Twenty-one

Two weeks later, Jack and Ashley were sunning themselves on the beach in Montauk, keeping a careful eye on John as he built a sandcastle close by.

"It feels good to finally get away," Ashley said softly, smiling as she watched her son's antics.

"You can say that again," Jack murmured, thinking about everything that had recently transpired. Drew Kaye had confessed to killing Frank Finnegan, after cutting a deal with the district attorney's office. The DA had agreed to seek a lesser charge of second-degree murder in exchange for the plea. With the evidence stacked against him, Kaye agreed to wave his right to a trial. He received a sentence of twenty-five years to life. Jack hoped that he never again saw the light of day.

"Come see what I did," John called out to them.

Jack smiled and rose to his feet, holding out his hand to Ashley. "Our son is calling us. Shall we?"

Ashley laughed and let Jack pull her from the sand. "Let's not keep him waiting."

"We're coming, pal," Jack called out to John as he and Ashley walked hand and hand over to where he played.

3/10